A HAUNTING IN ROSE GROVE

ROCKWELL SCOTT

Cover Art by The Cover Collection.

A HAUNTING IN ROSE GROVE

1

1995

Jake's parents told him they were moving into a new house, but the home in front of them could be called anything but new.

It was two stories tall and loomed solitary and foreboding, away from any other houses in Rose Grove.

"They say it's the largest house in town," Dad said, throwing an arm over Mom's shoulder. "And the oldest. Just needs a little fixing up."

Jake exchanged a glance with his brother Trevor. He was two years older than him — ten — and Jake always liked to check in with him in every situation. This time, Trevor shrugged.

"Why don't you boys look around the backyard?" Mom asked. "There should be plenty of room to play."

Jake and Trevor slinked off, Jake never taking his eyes off the house as he got nearer. The white paint was flaking off the base and even some windows were broken.

"When was the last time someone lived here?" Trevor wondered out loud.

"Why did we have to move at all?" Jake grumbled. Every night that week, Dad had tasked him with packing up his and Trevor's toys and belongings. It took forever.

"Hey, at least we don't have to change schools right before summer," Trevor said. Jake knew his brother was right. He'd had friends move away, and he never saw them again. He didn't want to be the kid that lost all his friends and had to make new ones. Especially so close to summer.

But he'd overheard Mom and Dad talking quietly about a "new addition" a few weeks ago. Jake realized that meant he would soon have a new baby brother or sister. Maybe that's why Dad felt they needed a bigger house.

As they approached the backyard, Trevor stopped suddenly beside him. "Wow!"

Jake followed his brother's gaze. There was a huge tree with the thickest trunk he'd ever seen with strong branches protruding about. In the lower, stronger branches, someone had built a tree house.

"I can't believe it!" Jake shouted.

The two boys ran to the base of the tree. Wooden planks were nailed into the trunk, a crude ladder in which to access the tree house.

Trevor went first as he always did. He hadn't made it one step before Dad intercepted.

"Whoa, now," he said. "No climbing up there until I've had a chance to inspect it."

"But Dad!" Trevor complained.

Dad's good temper melted away all at once. Jake and Trevor took a step back, knowing that darkened look quite well. It usually came without warning, and when it did, it was best to just shut up and agree.

"Boys, this tree house was built by the family before us, maybe even the one before them. I don't know how well they built it. I'll inspect it and make sure it's sturdy, but until then, neither of you are to go up there. Is that understood?"

Jake and Trevor both hung their heads in disappointment. "Yes, sir."

THE TREE HOUSE was a constant tease over the next few weeks. The family moved in and the renovations began, and as Jake predicted, the tree house was low on Dad's list of priorities. First, he worked on the pipes and plumbing, then the kitchen, then the painting and wallpaper.

What was worse, the tree house was visible from the bedroom that Jake and Trevor shared. It sat on top of the strong branch, eye level with their second story window. They talked about what they would do once they could finally go up there and how they would invite all of their friends over and what all they would put inside. Jake imagined himself giving it a makeover just like Mom and Dad were doing to the real house.

Then, one evening, close to the end of school, Jake overheard Mom imploring Dad. "You know summer is coming. The boys want to play in the tree house. Take one day and get it ready for them."

Dad, who had become stressed and irritable at all the house repairs, mumbled something in reply that Jake did not hear. He knew if Dad did not want to work on the tree house, he wouldn't, but Mom made a good argument.

Excited, Jake ran up to the bedroom and told his brother what he'd just overheard. The two were ecstatic.

Jake never witnessed Dad climb the tree and work on the tree house. Jake told himself that he did it while they were at school, and that he was not neglecting Mom's advice.

He clung tightly to these hopes. He and Trevor had already told all their friends around school that their new house had a *really cool* tree house, and all the boys were excited to come over and check it out.

Jake hoped it could hold them all.

Sure enough, when they came home from school on the last day, Dad met them at the door and said, "Boys, you're free to move into your second home."

Jake and Trevor let out a cry of excitement and rushed to the tree in the backyard. Trevor went first, just as he did weeks before when Dad had stopped them. They climbed high into the branches. As they ascended, Jake looked down, more frightened of heights than he thought he'd be. Still, after waiting so long, he forced himself to continue. Besides, his older brother was unaffected by the height, so he couldn't allow himself to be the only one too chicken to go up. Trevor's willingness to plow ahead gave him courage.

Once at the top, they entered the old tree house. It was built from wood and simple inside — three walls with windows and the fourth had the door. It looked like Dad had swept the inside.

Jake and Trevor spent the rest of the afternoon running back and forth between the tree house and their bedroom. They immediately transferred all the things they had planned to bring up there. An extra blanket to lie on the floor, a small table, a battery powered lamp and radio, and Trevor's comic book collection.

Mom watched as they worked, a smile on her face. "Boys, you can't take everything from the house and put it up the tree!"

They ignored her.

That evening, after the sun went down, the two brothers sat in their tree house, reading superhero comic books by flashlight, the radio playing alternative rock hits. Humidity left beads of sweat on Jake's temples, and the chirps of bugs and the hoots of night hunting birds sounded through the large backyard.

Jake leaned back against the wall, relaxed and comfortable. It was everything he had imagined it would be. Now summer could start in style.

Then the hairs on the back of Jake's neck stood and prickled. Jitters crawled down his spine, as if someone had come up behind him unseen. He sat forward and rubbed the skin around his shoulders, but he could not shake the feeling that someone was there. Trevor glanced at him, but said nothing.

He tried to settle back and relax, but the air to his left somehow felt *heavy,* as if someone was right there next to him, invading his personal space.

Jake's ear tickled, as if soft breath was slowly blown under the lobe. He stood and wiped his moist palms on his shorts, knowing that something was off.

"What's wrong?" Trevor asked.

"Nothing," Jake said. "Forget it."

This time he sat on the opposite side of the tree

house. He opened his comic again, but could not focus on the words. The heavy feeling was on his right side now, having followed him to the other side of the tree house.

"Are you done with that Batman?" Jake jumped, Trevor's sudden question startling him. "Whoa. Scared of the dark?"

"No," Jake shot back.

"No, you're not done with the Batman or no, you're not scared of the dark?"

Jake grimaced and tossed the comic to his brother. As he did, hot breath blew into his ear, and he squirmed away, brushing his ear lobe.

"What?" Trevor said.

"A bug keeps flying in there." Even though Jake knew that wasn't the case.

"Clean them out, then."

He ignored his brother's jibe and settled in next to him although there was plenty of room to spread out. Trevor did not comment on the proximity. Jake didn't pick up another comic, but instead gripped his flashlight tighter, slowly creeping the beam around the tree house. Half expecting to see a third person in there with them.

"I'm hungry," Trevor said, closing the Batman comic.

"We forgot to bring food up here." Jake frowned.

"I'll head down to grab something. Maybe some fruit snacks." Trevor stood and walked toward the tree house door. And Jake did not want to be left alone. Nerves clawed at his stomach as Trevor walked out onto the branch, gripping the limbs of the next highest branch to steady his balance.

Quit being a baby, he told himself. Trevor would laugh

at him if he admitted he didn't want to be by himself in the tree house.

But Jake's hand trembled as he held the flashlight. And even though he sweated from the humidity, chills spiked up his spine.

He stood and went to the door. "Trevor." His voice trembled.

His brother turned. "Yeah?"

Stop being stupid. He'll make fun of you.

"Nothing. Never mind."

The radio behind Jake, which had been playing an Oasis tune, turned suddenly to static.

"Adjust that antenna," Trevor said.

Jake turned and looked at it. The guitar riffs and vocals had turned into garbled nonsense. "Maybe it needs new batteries." He turned back to his brother. "Get some of those, too."

"Hmm, okay. Does it take double A's or —"

But Trevor never finished his thought. His body jerked backwards hard, flung off the branch, as if pushed. He screamed as he disappeared into the darkness. The next thing Jake heard was a loud thump as he landed hard on the ground.

"Trevor!" Jake hung his head out the door of the tree house, looking down. Through the dark night he could barely make out Trevor's crumpled form on the grass.

And his brother started to cry and scream in agony.

THE ONLY TIME Jake had been inside a hospital before was when Grandma had a bad case of pneumonia and had to stay for two nights. He, Mom, and Trevor had hung out in her room, watching her TV and playing with the remote control that made her bed move up and down and helping themselves to her desserts.

Now, Jake sank in the cushioned chair in the ER waiting room, watching Dad pace back and forth near the reception desk. He had the phone to his ear, stretching the cord as far as it would go, almost pulling it off the desk. The girl who sat there eyed it nervously.

"I'm telling you that's the wrong deductible," Dad barked down the line. "I'm not crazy. I know my policy." A long pause as he listened. "You're telling me you won't cover any more than that? That's insanity. What's the point of even having insurance?"

The door to the ER opened and Mom poked her head, then motioned for Jake to come. Then she glanced at Dad and rose her eyebrows, but he only shook his finger at her impatiently.

Jake followed Mom to ED 6, where she threw the curtain back. Trevor sat on the stretcher, and Jake hardly recognized him. His hair was sticking straight up, slicked with sweat and dirt. His eyes were wide, red, and puffy from crying. Tears had streaked through the grime on his cheeks.

And his right arm was wrapped in a tight blue cast and dangling in a black sling.

On the wall, a box of light held x-rays. One of them showed a nasty broken bone. The other was the same arm, but after the pieces had been put back together, like a puzzle.

A tall man in a white coat brushed past, holding a chart. "The post-reduction pictures look good," he told

Mom, nodding toward the x-rays. "We can discharge him and we'll see him back at our main orthopedic office in three weeks. You can make your appointment at the front desk."

"Thank you," Mom said.

"And be careful next time, Trevor," the doctor said, adopting a false, cheery voice. "No more falling out of tree houses."

He was pushed, Jake caught himself thinking.

The way Trevor had fallen... He'd been standing there, his feet sure. There was no lost balance, no flailing arms, no wide eyes or a sudden realization he was going overboard.

Just all of a sudden, his chest jerked and he fell backwards from a force that was much stronger than gravity.

Jake had seen kids pushed down on the playground at school dozens of times. Sometimes he had been the one who had been pushed. He knew what a boy looked like when he was pushed.

Trevor was shoved off that branch. He was sure of it.

But by what?

Although no one had been there that he could see, Jake had felt certain of a third presence inside the tree house, even though that seemed crazy.

And since he knew it sounded crazy, he told no one his theory. As far as everyone was concerned, Trevor fell and it was an accident.

2

2018

Boxes littered the floor in the living room, the kitchen, the hallway, and the bedroom.

Jake hated clutter. But as he stood with hands on hips and looked around the new apartment, trying to imagine what it would become, he couldn't help but smile. This time was different. It meant something more.

A large *thunk* from behind caused him to jump. Kelly had just dropped a box of kitchen supplies at her feet. A cloud of dust erupted from the floor. "I think that's the last of it."

He smiled. "Good. Let's get to unpacking."

Kelly sauntered into the living room and looked around, running a hand through her blonde hair. She tapped a box with the toe of her tennis shoe, lost in thought.

"You all right?" Jake asked, fearful of the answer.

"Yeah," Kelly said, her voice flat. "Just tired from

hauling boxes." She forced a smile and went over to him and pecked his lips. "And it'll take some getting used to."

Jake put his arms around her hips and pulled her close. "Thank you again for taking a chance."

She slapped his butt. "Come on. I can't feel calm while everything is in boxes." Kelly then disappeared into the bedroom.

Jake took a deep breath and let it out. Dust lingered in the air and tickled his nose. After a year and a half of dating, he was ready to move in together. However, when he'd broached the subject with Kelly, she wasn't as receptive as he thought she'd be.

Kelly had moved in immediately with her ex-boyfriend and the experience was less than good. Jake didn't know much about Greg, and didn't care to, but whatever had happened between them had put her off of living with her boyfriends.

But Jake was thirty-one years old and ready for stability and a place to call his own. The apartment he shared with two younger guys was no longer doing it for him, and he wanted his own home with his girlfriend.

He'd been able to convince Kelly to go along with the plan, but still he knew he was tip-toeing in uneasy territory.

Jake unloaded the kitchen supplies. The plates, cups, and utensils went into separate cabinets and drawers, and little by little, the kitchen came together.

As he worked, he realized the sounds of Kelly setting up their room had grown quiet.

"Kelly?" Jake called.

No answer. So he walked down the short hallway to the master bedroom.

She crouched on the floor near an open box, her back to him, looking at something in her hands.

"Kelly?" he asked again. "You all right?"

She turned and looked at him over her shoulder. Her blonde hair fell over her pink t-shirt.

"What's this? You've never shown this to me before."

Jake wondered what it could be. When he approached and saw what she had in her hands, his stomach sank.

It was a family photo. The only one he allowed himself to hold on to.

The faded, framed picture was of Mom and Dad and him and Trevor, when they were eight and ten years old. He'd forgotten he'd thrown it in the box. Kelly had never seen a photograph of his family before and he'd intended to keep it that way.

"Sorry," Jake sputtered. He reached out for the picture, but Kelly stood and kept it out of his grasp.

"No," Kelly said, looking at it again, studying it. "You never tell me anything about your family. And I want to know. Don't you think it's time?"

It was true. Jake did not talk about his family. What was the point? There was nothing but pain and history there. He had worked so hard in his teenage years and early twenties to get over all that shit, so why bring it up now?

Besides, half the people in that picture were dead, anyway.

"It's not something I talk about," he said simply. His voice was short and terse and he did not meet her eyes.

"Jake," she said, her face softening. "You have to tell me sometime. If we are going to do this, then I have to know you."

"This you don't want to know."

He reached out and took the picture from her hands and she let it go. He hated to exile her from this part of his life, especially after she'd taken a leap of faith and moved in with him. But for now, it was the only option, and it would be for a long time.

Family was just not something Jake had the luxury of having. Maybe he did once, but not anymore. He had worked very hard to accept that. He wished the other important people in his life could accept it too.

"You're my family now," he told her. "That's all you need to know, so don't worry about any of this."

And with that, he walked out of the room, taking the picture with him. For the life of him, he couldn't figure out why he kept it. Maybe because it was the only piece of memory left remaining of the Nolan family. Perhaps it was time to even let that go, just as he'd relinquished everything else.

Yet when Jake returned to the kitchen and held the frame over the trash can, he hesitated. He tried to make himself drop the picture inside, along with all the packaging garbage that had accumulated from their move.

But he couldn't do it.

Jake stared at the young face of his brother — smiling and happy and innocent. So full of joy. He slammed the photograph face down on the counter and shoved it away from him.

I have a new life to build.

One that would never cross paths with his past ever again.

3

After Jake disappeared from the bedroom with the picture, Kelly sighed. It was not the first time she had broached the subject and it would not be the last.

"Just talk to me," she whispered.

Everyone had a past. The two years she spent living with Greg were the worst of her life, and afterward she'd vowed never to live with another boyfriend again. She'd relented for Jake even though he knew how she felt. And yet he was still unwilling to meet her halfway in sharing his family trauma.

For as long as she'd known Jake, he was adamant about not talking about his family, as if he had a physical aversion. On their earliest dates, when it was normal to talk about such things, Kelly spilled all, telling him about her mother and father and how they split up, and how her two younger sisters were grown, with the youngest finishing college. She even told him about Butch, the family dog, who they'd recently put down.

But when Jake's turn came to input to the conversation, he deftly changed the subject. She'd noticed. He was good at it too. She could tell he was well practiced at avoiding family talk.

After a few dates, she finally got up the courage to ask why he never told her about his family. He'd simply smiled and said it was not something he ever talked about.

After three months, she brought Jake home to meet her mom and sisters and everything went well. They'd had a great weekend. But Jake made no indication he would ever take her to meet his family. That bothered her, and when she brought it up at five months, it was the first time he became angry with her.

Perhaps not angry. He was just avoidant.

"I do not have a family," he'd said, his voice flat and deep. "There is no one for you to meet and nowhere for us to go. My parents are dead, and my brother is gone."

She figured there was some type of trauma in the past, something not dealt with that he was reluctant to bring up.

It broke her heart that his parents had died. They must have passed young. But it was the other part that gave her pause.

My brother is gone.

What did that mean, exactly?

Kelly resumed unpacking her clothes from the boxes and hanging them in the closet. As she worked, though, she could not get the family photograph out of her mind. It was the first time she'd ever seen his family, and honestly she was surprised Jake kept it. She'd never seen it before, which meant that he'd hidden it in his old apartment.

But if this relationship was going to work out in the long run, she had to know what happened to him in the past. Traumas not dealt with were a poison in future relationships and marriages — she'd learned that from her time with Greg. That guy was a bundle of baggage and too macho to deal with it correctly.

And she did not want to have history repeat itself with Jake. He was a good man, and the last thing she wanted was to see him tormented by whatever he assumed was too powerful to ever let go of.

It took two weeks before the new apartment finally became a home. The furniture was in place, the bedroom set up and decorated, the refrigerator stocked. They had even been cooking in their kitchen. When Kelly came back from work after a long day of teaching young children, she walked in and felt relaxed. At home. In a sanctuary.

She could kick off her shoes and feel the carpet on her bare feet, prop her legs on the coffee table if she wanted. There was a television and a bookshelf with books — her favorite ones that she had kept and some that she had not started, her to-be-read stack always piling up and never getting any smaller. The bathroom was small, but clean, with a nice tub where she could drop in a bath bomb and soak.

Maybe her reluctance to move in had been misplaced. Perhaps Jake was the key factor that brought it all together.

But something still nagged at her thoughts.

You're my family now, he had told her. That was sweet and all, and she did not mind being there for him, but before long she needed to know what happened to him.

One day, when Kelly had the place to herself for an hour before Jake returned from work, she grabbed her computer and opened a search tab.

Trevor Nolan, she typed.

There were many Trevor Nolans in the world. She scrolled the first pew pages of search results but couldn't find one that would obviously be Jake's brother.

His parents are dead, but his brother is gone.

She deleted her search and started over.

Trevor Nolan Rose Grove Georgia.

Jake had mentioned the small town of his youth a few times. Kelly remembered because she thought it sounded quaint and adorable.

The first link led to the Rose Grove local newspaper's website.

Rose Grove's prodigal son returns.

Dated three months before, it told the story of how Trevor Nolan, who once lived in Rose Grove, had returned to the town and purchased his childhood home for him and his family.

Below the article was a picture. Trevor Nolan was no longer the boy in the photograph she'd seen. He was tall, much broader than Jake, and though only two years older, he appeared far more aged. Only a ring of hair around the perimeter of his head remained. His wife was a plump lady who posed beside him and several inches shorter, smiling just as big as him. Between them stood a young boy of about eight or nine.

Kelly studied the picture. Although they looked very

different, the mouths and eyes were the same. This man was definitely Jake's brother.

He isn't gone. He just went back home. Literally.

The article detailed how the Nolans had lived in the house when Trevor was younger before moving out two years later. Now, Trevor had returned to town and purchased the house for his new family.

"I can't wait to introduce my wife and son to this wonderful place," Trevor was quoted. "Of course, it will take some fixing up, but we're ready for the challenge. My father did the same when we first moved in, and I'm excited to begin work. Except this time I get to choose my bedroom!"

The end of the article talked about the home and how it was the oldest standing house in Rose Grove, built before Rose Grove was declared a town in the early 1800s.

Kelly smiled to herself. Moving into your childhood house and fixing it up for your new family? It was perfect for a small town newspaper story.

But would Jake feel the same?

Would he be happy to hear that his brother was doing well? That she found him? Was he already aware about this? Did he keep up with Trevor at all?

She had no idea about any of it.

But she knew what she needed to do. She would ask him, and judging by his reaction, she would decide if this would be the last time she ever brought it up.

One final attempt to learn the truth about her boyfriend's past.

When Jake returned from work an hour later, she kissed him at the door before he went into the bedroom to change into sweatpants. They cooked dinner together and talked about their days as they ate. Jake's boss was pleased with the project he'd turned in and promised that the promotion was around the corner. Kelly brought up Bryson as she usually did — the problem child that terrorized her classroom. There were most likely problems going on at home, so she couldn't get too mad at him.

They washed the dishes and settled in front of the television to flick through the channels. It was then that Kelly made her move.

"I did some research on the Internet today."

"Oh. About what?"

"About... Trevor."

Jake's head snapped over to her. His face was exactly what she'd been expecting — surprise and even a little anger.

"Here," she said quickly, grabbing her computer and opening it. "I want you to read this."

"I don't want to." He tried to stand up from the couch, but Kelly grabbed his arm and stopped him from leaving.

"No. Please look. Only this one thing. If you do, I promise I'll never bring it up again."

Jake considered her deal and then rejoined her on the couch. His hands wrung together in his lap.

Just what the hell happened back then?

She handed Jake the computer with the article pulled up. He took it from her as if it was going to burn him, and the brave face he wore was nothing more than a false mask. Kelly knew he was desperate to remain collected.

She watched him as he read the story. Although the

light in the room was dim from the single lamp, she saw the color drain from Jake's face. His lips moved, his eyes widening as they darted across the screen.

She recognized from his reaction that he had not seen this article and did not keep up with his brother's comings and goings. He did not know about him purchasing the childhood home.

When he finished, Jake slowly closed the laptop and stared into a fixed place on the floor.

"I thought it was a sweet story," Kelly said, more to break the silence than anything else. "I mean… check out the family picture. They all look so happy."

Jake did not answer. Only continued to stare. Tears formed in the corners of his eyes.

"Jake?"

"Excuse me," he said, standing and walking to the bedroom.

"Where are you going?"

"I just need a minute, please."

The bedroom door closed softly behind him.

4

Jake paced back and forth in the bedroom. His heart pounded and sweat broke out all over his body.

Why did Kelly have to bring it up again?

Why did she think he never considered searching his brother's name? It was Google, so of course he would find him if he tried.

Trevor looked similar to when Jake saw him last, but still older. His brother was aging must faster than him, looking closer to forty-three than thirty-three. He was also out of shape and not maintaining his health.

Six years ago, he married Linda. It was the only instance Jake ever succumbed to the temptation to Google his brother. He'd found the engagement announcement and decided to show up.

Jake did not know what he was thinking at the time. Maybe he was hoping to use the gravity of such a momentous occasion to reconnect with Trevor. So, without much consideration, he got his suit resized and drove to the wedding ceremony. There, he watched his brother get married while standing in the back of the church. No one even noticed him.

When it was time for the couple to walk out with the few guests in attendance seeing them off, Jake joined them. As they walked, the people clapped — less a cheer and more like something you'd see in a game of golf — and Trevor and Linda were thrilled. Until Trevor laid eyes on Jake.

At first, it took him a minute to recognize him. Trevor halted in his tracks, his wife pulled backwards since her arm was linked through his. Linda looked between the pair of them, trying to figure out just who the stranger was. Trevor must not have spoken of him or shown her a picture.

"You have to go," was all that Trevor said. "Please. You are not welcome here."

Then, his brother got into the car with his new bride and they drove away. The crowd from the wedding dissipated and Jake stood there alone outside the church.

Afterward, Jake regretted going. If Trevor wanted him there, then he would have contacted him. He could not force his brother to speak to him. And besides, was Jake even sure that he himself wanted to reconcile? Maybe things were best the way they were.

So Jake loosened his tie and drove home and vowed to never contact Trevor again. It was just too painful.

Now that Kelly had drudged up the past, she found something far worse than a wedding announcement.

Trevor had gone back to that house.

And he brought his wife and child there.

For what reason? Why? Jake's heart pounded in his

chest. There could be *no* explanation. That horrible place killed their parents. Destroyed their family. Nearly ruined him.

And Jake wasn't even the one most affected.

JAKE WAS in the bedroom for a long time. Kelly bit her lip and wrung her hands, waiting for him to come out. She now knew this was a trauma she could never fix. He needed professional help. Whatever lurked in his past and could disarm her usually strong boyfriend was too great and out of her control.

While she waited, Kelly sat and opened her computer again. She clicked away from the article about the new home purchase and searched Trevor Nolan again.

Many sites came up that were not what she was looking for. Then she found another picture of him, different from the one in the Rose Grove newspaper. He looked at the camera with a three quarters turn and cast a solemn, heavy stare at the viewer, his mouth a firm, straight line — an odd foil to the beaming happy photograph from the article.

Kelly followed the link to a shoddy website for a group called Spirit Seekers, a paranormal investigation team.

What?

Trevor Nolan's headshot appeared among two other guys on the page listing the members. She clicked on the picture and Trevor's section of the site loaded.

HEY THERE. My name is Trevor and I'm a banker. In my spare time, though, I like to investigate the paranormal. I love researching, reading about, and getting my hands on anything haunted. If you're interested as well, check out my blog, where I talk about interesting cases I've discovered or experienced. Hope you enjoy!

KELLY CLICKED on the link to the blog. It was not updated often and the posts were long and drawn out and not well written. They were usually named something like "The Case of Such-and-Such House" where Trevor would write about a haunted house and the family who lived there and what they experienced. Sometimes the ghosts were friendly, other times less so. Every post had white text over a black background.

It was definitely the work of an amateur — a part time enthusiast.

What a strange side gig. Paranormal investigator?

Did he actually investigate the hauntings? Or did he just browse stuff on the Internet that he considered interesting? Kelly had seen those ghost shows on television where the guys brought in equipment to the haunted places and tried to catch voices on recordings. Then one single bump in the night would send them all running away. Hardly the professionals.

The latest entry on the blog, dated three months ago, gave Kelly pause.

HEY FRIENDS. I've been silent here lately, but I have news! I recently purchased my childhood home in Rose Grove, Georgia, for myself and my family. We will move in soon. Renovations are needed, but it's a job I look forward to.

Some of you who know me personally have already heard about this house, but for those of you who do not, let me fill you in. This place is haunted and has been since before I moved in when I was a child. So many weird things happened, in fact, that we had to move out. After, my family fell apart and was never the same. I blame this house for causing the early deaths of my parents.

Knowing what I do about the paranormal, the fixing up on this place won't just be painting and replacing the plumbing. No, I plan to kick this ghost out of these walls. Send it back to wherever it came from.

Show it that I am no longer afraid of it.

I will update my progress regularly on this blog. Follow along, and as always, if you have any questions or comments, please leave them below.

"Oh my god," Kelly whispered. Was this real?

There was nothing else on the blog. Normally she would have thought these were the ramblings of a crazy guy, but after seeing how Jake reacted whenever his brother was mentioned, her mind was open to anything.

Not trauma. Not abuse.

They were haunted?

5

Twenty minutes later, Jake walked back into the room, having composed himself as best he could.

"I'm sorry," Kelly said.

Jake waved his hand at her. "Please. I've asked you to not talk about my family."

"I understand," Kelly said. "But there's more."

Jake looked up at her. His eyes were wide, mouth dry. Kelly looked back at him as if frightened of what he might do next. "What do you mean?"

"Something else you should probably see." She gestured toward the computer on the coffee table.

Jake sat beside her and stared at the machine like it was a snake ready to bite him. "I'm not sure I can look at anything else. I don't want to know."

What is this? I've worked so hard to leave it behind. Then in one single night it all comes back.

"Do you still care about your brother?" Kelly asked him.

The question caught him off guard. "I don't know. He doesn't feel the same about me, but I guess I want to rebuild something. He's the only family I have left."

"If you think there will ever be a future, then you need to read what I found."

Jake swallowed hard as Kelly handed him the computer. Jake's eyes flicked over the strange, black website, resting on the headshot of his brother, the very serious gaze staring back at him.

"What am I looking at? Paranormal investigator?"

"Your brother has a hobby on the side," Kelly told him.

"Oh my god." Jake scrolled around the site. *You idiot. What have you been up to?*

"What you need to see is on the last page. The blog post."

Jake clicked and read it quickly. "What the hell? No… That can't be right."

"This thing that happened to your family. You were haunted, weren't you?"

Jake looked at his girlfriend. She seemed so concerned about him — almost afraid. "Do you believe in ghosts?" he heard himself asking.

Kelly licked her lips and tucked a loose piece of hair behind her ear. "Umm."

"Forget it," he snapped, shooting up from the couch. How could he have ever imagined he'd want to talk about this?

But Kelly grabbed him and pulled him back down. "Please tell me. I'll listen to anything you say. No judgement."

Jake took a deep breath and steadied himself. He'd

never spoken of this before. Anyone who heard his story would think he was insane.

"That house we lived in when we were kids." He pointed toward the computer where the article was still pulled up in a tab. "There was something there. Something not *right.* It terrorized us. Made my father crazy and my mother depressed. It tore us apart. After that, nothing was ever the same."

"What happened?" Kelly asked.

And Jake's mind raced back through all the terrible memories. All beginning with the night his brother was pushed from the tree.

"It's too much to tell," Jake said. He avoided meeting her eyes.

Kelly took his hand and held it. "I'm sorry to bring this up. It's just that I care about you and I want to learn how I can help you."

He squeezed her hand. "You can't."

"And what about your brother? Can you help him?"

Jake closed his eyes and ground his teeth. *Leave it. Let it go. It's his own life, and he doesn't want me in it.*

"Jake?" Kelly asked.

But Jake remembered that summer too well. No matter how much he tried to forget it. Those had been the months when his and Trevor's rolls reversed. Trevor had always been the older one who Jake looked up to and wanted to emulate. After that summer, all of that had changed. Jake had become his rock, the one who tried to reassure him that everything would be all right, even when he didn't know if that was true.

Should I be his rock one more time? No one else understands what happened in that house...

Trevor had been the one to shut him out. Refused to reconcile. But Trevor had always been stubborn, and Jake knew that if his brother stayed in the house long enough, he would eventually share the same fate as their parents. And Jake couldn't sit by and let that happen without trying.

"I have to go," he said.

"Go where?"

"Home." Not being invited to his wedding was inconsequential, but this was something else entirely. "Trevor cannot do this. I can't sit here while he moves his family into that house. He knows how dangerous it is! He has a little kid for crying out loud."

Kelly put her hands on his arm but it did nothing to calm him. "Jake, please tell me what you need me to do."

Jake shook his head. He grabbed Kelly's computer and brought up an airfare search engine.

"You're going now?" Kelly asked.

"I have to. The longer I wait, the worse it will get. He's already been there for three months." He searched flights to Atlanta.

Kelly, not sure what to do, watched him in silence. Jake understood he was acting like a crazy person, but the situation was desperate. He found one that departed the next day and booked it without looking at the price.

"Do you want me to come with you?" Kelly offered.

"Absolutely not. It's too dangerous."

"What should I do?"

"Wait here."

Now it was Kelly's turn to get upset. "I can't do that. You just told me it's dangerous, but you're running off alone?"

"You don't even believe in hauntings!" Jake took his cell phone from his pocket and dialed.

"Who are you calling?"

"My boss."

The conversation with Mr. Allen only lasted a few minutes. Jake apologized for bothering him at home, explained there was a family emergency, and that he would be out of town for a few days, although he didn't know when he'd be back.

"Are you absolutely sure you have to go?" Mr. Allen asked. "You know it's a crazy time around the office. All these new clients…"

"I understand," Jake said, hearing the subtle hint that his departure could affect his shot at the promotion he was currently working toward. In the end, Mr. Allen reluctantly agreed.

"Thank you," Jake said. "And again, I'm sorry, but this is urgent and I have to take care of it."

When he hung up, Kelly asked, "What about the promotion?"

Before Jake could answer, something fell from the ceiling into Kelly's lap — a huge, brown cockroach.

She screamed and stood up, brushing the thing off of her. And Jake felt a chill course through his entire body, frozen in place.

The bug scurried across the carpet.

"Get it, Jake!" Kelly shouted.

"No," he said calmly. "It'll disappear."

It's happening again.

"What?" Kelly looked at him, confused. "What are you talking about? Kill it!"

The cockroach disappeared underneath the cushioned

chair pushed against the wall on the far side of the room. Jake lifted the chair.

It had vanished into thin air.

"How..." Kelly was terrified.

Jake remembered the cockroaches all too well. *The ghost's calling card.* "As I said, I have to go. It's happening again."

6

1995

"*Hut!*" Jason barked.

Jake sprinted forward, zigged past Brian, zagged away from Peter, and broke free into the open field beyond. He twisted and met eyes with Jason, playing QB, who wound back and hurled the ball right toward him. It was low, so Jake dropped to catch, but the ball hit the dust before bouncing into his arms.

"Come on, Jake!" Jason shouted.

"Don't throw it low!" he shot back, tossing the ball back to his friend.

Jason caught it easily. "You have to get under it. Trevor could've had that one."

Jake glanced to his right. Trevor sat on the park bench staring at the pickup game, but not really seeing. He didn't move, cheer, or shout from the sidelines. His arm hung lamely in the sling.

Jason was right, though. Trevor could've caught that. Which meant Jake wanted to prove he could do it too.

"Throw it to me again," he whispered to Jason as the boys lined up again, and Jason nodded.

"*Hut*!"

Jake took off again. After the last play, Brian was more wary of him and covered him better, but Jake was faster. He pulled away from the other kid and once again found open field. He turned just in time to see Jason lean back and throw the football. Jake judged the lead the ball had on him, kept his speed, and the wobbly spiral landed right into his waiting arms like two magnets coming together. He ran it into the area they'd designated as the end zone, the cheers of his team mates howling in the distance.

Jake held up the football, wide smile on his face. The first place he looked was to the sideline, but his brother was gone. And suddenly the thrill of his touchdown reception fizzled.

Jake returned home that evening dirty and sweaty and out of breath. He found Trevor alone on the couch, blanket up to his chin, watching television in the dark.

"Where did you go? Did you see my touchdown catch earlier?"

Trevor only grunted.

"Oh man," Jake went on. "Brian was trying to cover me but I'm way too fast for him. Which is crazy because I remember last year he used to be faster than me. But anyway, it was right into my hands and I ran it in. I wish you had seen it."

Trevor took his hand from beneath the blanket, aimed the remote at the screen, and turned the volume up several notches, way too loud.

Jake got the hint. He trudged to the stairs and up to his bedroom. As he went, Dad was in the dining room, on the ladder, using a screwdriver on the light in the ceiling. "Goddammit," he said through gritted teeth.

"Harry! Language!" Mom implored from the kitchen.

The next day, around ten o'clock, there was a knock on the door. Jake answered it to find Jason standing on his porch, football in hand.

"Bret wants a rematch," Jason explained. "Come on!"

"Uhh. One minute."

Jake left Jason standing there, confused. He went to the living room, where Trevor watched cartoons on the couch. "Jason is here. Do you want to come to the park and play football?"

"I can't play," Trevor said, voice flat and empty.

"I know but… you can watch."

"Where's the fun in that? You go."

But Jake felt guilty leaving his brother all alone in the house all day. So he went back to Jason and said, "I'll meet you guys there later." Even though he had no intention of doing so.

"What? The game starts now! We need you."

"Just give me some time. I can't play right now."

Jason groaned, but he eventually left.

Jake returned to the couch and watched cartoons with his brother. He would've much preferred to be out playing football, but he knew if the rolls were reversed, Trevor would have done the same for him. Even though he couldn't understand why his brother didn't even want to watch. Or leave the house. That was very unlike him.

Late in the afternoon, Jake watched the sun descend over the treetops through the living room window.

They'd spent all day watching television. "Trevor, can we go do something outside now?"

"I want to watch this."

Dad burst through the front door, home from work and tearing open a piece of mail. Mom greeted him at the door, but said nothing when she saw his scowl.

"Look at this," he said, shoving the paper in her face. Before she could read it properly, he said, "These hospital bills are through the roof. We can't afford something like this."

Jake knew this wasn't a conversation they should be hearing, but Dad didn't seem bothered that they were within earshot.

Mom kept her voice calm. "This is not something we could have predicted. It was an accident. We'll get through it."

"Damn tree house. Should have known better than to let those boneheads climb up there."

Jake glanced at Trevor, who only frowned and pretended like he didn't hear.

Jake agreed with Dad. If the tree house had not existed, Trevor never would have fallen. If he hadn't fallen, then he might not be acting so weird.

Mom cast a short glance toward Jake and Trevor. "Harry..."

Dad turned to them as if seeing them for the first time. "Have you two been watching TV all day?"

"Trevor doesn't feel like playing with his hurt arm," Mom explained.

Dad only rolled his eyes and grumbled something under his breath. He disappeared upstairs without another word.

A commercial came on. Trevor flipped to a different channel and started watching that one instead.

ONE NIGHT, three weeks after Trevor had fallen, the two of them were in their room, having already gotten ready for bed. It was nine o'clock and their parents had gone to sleep.

Trevor said, "Jake?"

Jake looked over at his brother. "Yeah?"

"Can you do me a favor?"

"Sure." He sat up straight. Trevor rarely asked him for favors.

"I want to read my comic books. But we left them. You know… up there."

Jake frowned.

He had not been up in the tree house since that night, nor did he want to go. The height had made him nervous the first time, but Trevor had given him strength. Going alone — and in the dark — would be completely different.

And what if he was pushed out of the tree, too? What if he also broke a bone? Dad would be very upset.

"Please?" Trevor asked.

Jake already knew he was going to go no matter what. He would do anything for his brother because Trevor would do anything for him.

So he pulled on his shoes and went downstairs and outside in his pajamas.

The night was dark and the moon shrouded in clouds. A heavy wind blew the leaves of the big tree, making the branches sway as if they were alive. A summer storm was brewing and would probably hit soon.

Jake stood at the base of the trunk, looking up. He wiped his sweaty palms on his pajamas. He wasn't sure if he was more frightened of the heights or of being pushed from the tree. It was as if the tree house — or the tree itself — did not want him there.

He tried to convince himself those were silly thoughts.

I'll only be up there for a second. Just long enough to grab the comic books and come back down.

Jake put his foot on the first rung and hoisted himself up. Then he paused and looked at the house. Everything was dark except for the upstairs window of his bedroom. Trevor's silhouette stood gazing at him.

Although Dad had not explicitly told them they were forbidden from the tree house, Jake understood that if he caught him going up there alone at night, then he would be in huge trouble.

But Trevor needed his comics.

So Jake climbed. One rung at a time. He made sure he had a grip on each new step before hoisting himself up. As he progressed, he sensed the ground disappearing from beneath him, dipping further and further away.

It seemed like forever had passed before he reached the thick branch that held the tree house. Jake shuffled slowly on it, surprised by how dark it was that night. He didn't have a flashlight like the first time, and with the new moon, everything was cast in black. His only flashlight was still in the tree house.

Jake crouched down and crawled along the rough bark on his hands and knees. He did not want to balance on his feet alone. He had to grope his way to the entrance rather than rely on his eyes.

Eventually, he found the door. The interior was even darker than outside, and everything inside was still the way they'd left it. He grabbed the flashlight they had used to read. He snatched it up and switched it on. Nothing. It did not work.

Jake shook it and tried a few more times, clicking it on and off. Strange. They had just changed the batteries that first night and it had worked fine then.

He set it down and grabbed the flashlight Trevor had been using. Clicked it on. Same thing. He was stuck with the darkness.

Forget it. All I have to do is grab the comics and go.

He fumbled with his hands until he found them. He put them in a neat stack that he tucked under his arm.

That was when Jake got the impression that he was not alone.

He whirled toward the tree house door where he thought the presence came from. But there was nothing there. Only darkness.

He looked out the tree house window to his bedroom. Perhaps the eyes were Trevor's. But Trevor was no longer there.

No one to watch over him.

Jake's breath turned to pants. His sudden anxiety had little to do with the heights — he felt like something was in there with him, even though he couldn't see anything.

So he rushed to the tree house door and stood on the edge. How could he crawl while still holding the comic books? If he shuffled too fast, he might fall. If he crept too slow, he risked being shoved.

Then he heard sounds behind him. A whispering voice.

He didn't want to turn around, but he did anyway.

He saw it there, floating where he had just been standing.

It was a black mass, darker than the surrounding night. It resembled billowing smoke, but the form was roughly human, a hazy shadow that would scatter in the wind.

Jake sensed a very strong emotion coming from it, one that made him sadder than he'd ever felt — worse than the times he'd fought with Trevor or when his parents fought in front of him. This *thing* seemed to be able to ball those emotions up and plant them straight into Jake's chest.

Jake froze in place, unable to look away. He tried to scream but nothing came out. His throat was closed and locked and not even his breath could break through. Although the black mass did not have eyes, Jake knew it was glaring at him, that it was the thing he had sensed inside the tree house with him.

This was what pushed Trevor.

It did not want him there. Jake couldn't explain how he knew it, but he understood the message surely within his heart.

When Jake finally found control of his body again, he dropped the comic books off the side and turned to rush down the tree branch. Trembling, he navigated his way with his knees and hands as fast as he could. Tears streamed down his face.

Please don't push me. Please don't make me fall. I'm leaving. And I'll never come back. I promise.

Jake found the trunk after what seemed like crawling for miles. The hair on the back of his neck stood up, as if the black shadow was following right behind him, chasing him away. He gripped the ladder and rushed down.

He wasn't sure how far from the ground he was, but he didn't care. He let go and fell the rest of the way. He tumbled further than he thought, having misjudged the distance, and landed hard. Pain shot through his feet and ankles and he crashed onto his side, hitting his head on the dirt.

He got up, though, ignoring the pain, and scooped up the comics he had dropped from above. Then he ran back into the house and up to the bedroom.

He threw the comics on Trevor's bed and collapsed onto his own, panting and crying and gasping for air. Sweat dripped from his temples and a dull ache pulsed in his legs and head from the fall.

"What happened to you?" Trevor asked.

Jake took a few seconds to get his breathing under control. "I saw something. In the tree house," he managed between breaths.

Trevor gave him a strange look. "Maybe an owl?"

"No," Jake said. "Something…" But he couldn't describe what he'd seen. A shadow shaped like a man, but shadows were always cast by something real, and nothing had been there. Besides, there was no light. It was just some sort of monster.

And he definitely didn't know how to articulate the feeling it gave him — that it wanted him gone immediately, otherwise it would force him.

"Forget it," Jake said.

Trevor shrugged and opened a comic book.

Jake went to the window and drew the curtain, blocking the old tree house from view. Long after Trevor turned off the lights, Jake was still wide awake.

Every time he closed his eyes, he saw that black mass.

And he promised himself he'd never go into the tree house again.

7

2018

The plane trembled during the turbulence. The fasten seatbelt light lit up and the captain came over the loudspeaker to warn the passengers of what they already knew.

Jake gripped both armrests. He hated flying, and he despised turbulence even more. It had always freaked him out. How did a thing so huge stay in the air like that?

His headphones were in and he watched a movie in the back of the headrest of the seat in front of him — some stupid comedy he had already forgotten the name of and that wasn't particularly funny. He only watched it to distract himself, hoping the rest of the flight would even out and go smooth.

Then his screen changed.

It fizzled and garbled. Static like a bad connection. Which was weird because the movies were in the software

— not streamed or broadcasted from anywhere. There should be no interruption to their playback.

Jake tapped the screen a few times, and it straightened out. But a minute later, the static returned. Lines blinked on the screen and the voices of the actors garbled in his headset.

He checked the passenger next to him. His screen was working fine. He looked between the seats at the two in front of him — those screens also worked.

His display continued to distort until the entire image disappeared. Then, the voices changed.

A deep, dark voice. At first unclear, it slowly crystalized as the same word repeated itself over and over in his ears.

"Don't."

"Don't."

"Don't!"

The last one was so loud that Jake ripped the headphones from his head and the screen turned black. When Jake tried to turn it back on, it did not work.

Jake trembled in his seat, a cold sweat covering his entire body.

That thing from the house.

It had happened before when he was eight. The first time, it had been the radio right before Trevor was pushed. No matter where Jake was, the thing remembered.

It must know he was coming. And it was not happy.

Jake knew this was a warning.

THE PLANE LANDED and Jake realized every step forward in the airport was defying the warning he had been given.

He looked around and over his shoulder, probably appearing to others like a paranoid person.

He wasn't sure what he was looking for — he could never know. The thing could take on any form. The black blob in the air was the first he had seen in his youth, but that was only one of the many guises. Whatever was needed at the time to serve its purpose.

And it could appear anywhere and at anytime.

Jake grabbed his bag from the conveyer belt and made his way to the help desk to rent a car. They gave him one with a GPS and, when he got inside, he typed in the address he still had memorized from his childhood.

The navigation system calculated the route and drew the line straight to Rose Grove, then informed him the drive would take about an hour and forty-five minutes.

Jake fought traffic getting out of Atlanta. Then, he took an exit off the Interstate and onto the old country highway that would bring him all the way to his childhood home.

As he drove, his grip tightened on the steering wheel. He felt a heaviness in his heart that seemed strong enough to crush him. A headache bloomed between his eyes. He had underestimated the anxiety he would feel just being an hour away from the place that held so many traumatic memories.

How could Trevor ever *live* there? Hopefully he would get all the answers soon.

As Jake traveled down the road, he saw a shape form in the distance. At first it was a black shadow, but as it drew closer, he realized it was a motorcycle coming his way. Except it was driving in his lane, speeding toward him.

"Dumb kid," he muttered.

But, as the two vehicles neared each other, he understood that the motorcyclist wasn't going to shift back into his correct lane.

At least, not until the last moment. Like a stupid, dangerous game of chicken.

Jake shifted the car a little to the left, not in the mood to play the ego game and wanting to let the kid just win.

But as he moved, the motorcyclist did as well. Lining himself up to be head on with him again. And made no further effort to correct his course.

"What are you doing?" Jake muttered. He drifted back into the correct lane, but was blocked by the motorcycle again. Perfect mirror movements. The rider was dressed all in black, with a tinted helmet and black gloves, still as a statue on top of the bike.

We're going to crash.

But something seemed off.

No roaring engine. No revving. Completely silent.

It's not real!

Jake gripped the wheel and closed his eyes. But no crash came.

When he opened them again, there was nothing ahead of him but open road. No one was in his rearview mirror.

It had gone straight through him, then vanished.

Jake let out the long, trembling breath he'd been holding.

Not even there and I'm already under attack.

It wanted him to spin out of control, flip his car, or

crash. The thing would be aggressive. And this time they would play for keeps.

8

Rose Grove, Georgia had grown since Jake had seen it last. They had lived there for about two years before the family had moved — before they had been forced to move.

The streets were all the same, and many of the familiar shops were still there. There were also some new ones. A Wal-Mart had come to town and a neighborhood had sprung up on the far end of Main Street, which before had been nothing but forest. He and Trevor used to play there when they were kids — after Trevor's arm healed and they both feared the tree house.

As Jake took the small turns in the cramped downtown, he turned off the GPS, finding he remembered the way home just fine.

There was a single road that branched off one of the main drags of town, and it continued in a long, curvy path through a heavily wooded area until it opened up to the large property where their house had been.

Jake expected that the trees would have been torn

down and replaced by more houses or developments, maybe some shops. But no. There were the same old oak trees that had been there before. Their branches draped over the road, a bit too deep. They would scratch the roofs of cars that were too tall. Thick, grey moss hung like curtains that led to another world.

And then, when Jake came around the last curve, the house of his childhood appeared ahead of him.

And he slammed on the brakes. A cloud of dust kicked up from his tires and drifted into the air.

Jake sat there for a long time in his idling car, staring at it. His chest tightened, making his next breaths difficult. Every fiber in his body told him to turn tail and flee. Told him he was stupid to return after he'd already escaped. Told him he and his family had paid too high a price for living there before, and that if Trevor was dumb enough to bring his own family there, then let it be.

But he had to fight those feelings.

Jake eased the car closer. He pulled to the right and parked in the same place his parents used to park their cars. His rental was the only vehicle there, which meant it was likely no one was home.

Even though he'd moved in three months ago, Trevor had made little progress with the renovations. The house was still painted white — the color that Dad had chosen. But the paint was peeling and flaking, cracked and crumbling. Dirt and black and brown smudges also marred the finish. The wood of the wraparound porch was warped and discolored, probably needing to be ripped up and replaced entirely. Mom had loved that porch.

Jake walked around the right side of the house. The windows that looked into the living room were dark, almost black, as if tinted. Jake could only see his own reflection in them.

The house was completely silent. There was no wind, so the leaves in the surrounding trees did not rustle. No birds chirped. The only sound was the crunch of grass and dirt underneath Jake's foot.

As he walked, Jake realized where he was instinctively headed. *Is it still there? Or maybe whatever family owned the place after us cut it down?*

No. It looked exactly as he remembered — the thick trunk and gnarled roots that dipped under and above the ground. As Jake approached, nausea coursed through his stomach. Even though he was grown, the tree still seemed so huge, like a monster that tormented him.

The wooden planks in the trunk remained. They had never been replaced and were brown and moldy, having survived many rainstorms. Jake touched the first rung of the ladder and the corner of the plank melted into his hand. He rubbed the soft splinters between his fingertips and they rained to the ground.

The tree house stood just as it had before, except now the wood was dark and discolored. If Dad had been nervous about the durability of the structure when they moved in, he would have for sure forbidden them from going up there now. It looked as if the next very strong wind would knock the thing out of the branch and send it tumbling to the ground.

If so, then good riddance.

He looked over this shoulder and found the window of his childhood bedroom. It was mostly blocked from view. The limbs of the tree had grown thick and unruly and the farthest reaching ones scratched the walls of the house. There were marks in the paint around the window — and scratches in glass — from where the branches scraped during windy days like the claws of a giant beast.

Jake heard a car arrive at the front, the rocks and dirt crunching underneath the tires. The engine was killed, followed by car doors and low voices. Probably wondering who the strange car belonged to.

Butterflies appeared in Jake's stomach and his limbs turned to lead. He had not felt that way since waiting for his last job interview to begin. There was no telling how his brother would react to his being there.

Jake mustered his courage and walked around the side of the house. Both Trevor and his wife Linda looked exactly as they had in the photograph in the newspaper. The two of them inspected the mysterious car, Trevor scratching his bald spot. Their son stood with them.

Linda spotted him first. "Trevor," she said nervously, never taking her eyes off of him. She did not remember him.

Trevor turned and their eyes met. At first, it took him a moment to recognize who Jake was, but then that realization set in. His mouth became a thin, terse line. "Linda, go inside."

"Is that Jake?" Linda asked her husband.

"Linda. Please take Daniel and go inside."

Daniel noticed his father's demeanor and hid behind Linda's leg. She threw a protective arm over him.

"But Trev — "

"Linda." He spoke through clenched teeth.

With no further argument, Linda grabbed Daniel's hand and the two of them walked up the porch and went inside, the screen door squeaking on its hinges. Jake heard Daniel say, "Mama, who is that?"

Jake and Trevor faced each other as if in a standoff. As if at any moment, one of them would draw an unseen pistol and shoot the other. Judging by Trevor's expression, he looked like he wanted to.

"What are you doing here?" Trevor asked.

Jake studied him for a long time before answering. His brother's face had aged considerably, and he appeared ten years older than he was. The extra weight around his gut didn't help. His skin was lined with wrinkles and bags, as if he'd lived with constant stress, struggle and worry. Perhaps he had. Jake would have no way of knowing. "I think you know."

Trevor glared at him. "You shouldn't be here."

"I didn't want to come," Jake told him. "You made it very clear at your wedding we were through, and I was prepared to let it be forever. But this is too far. You can't do this."

"It's too late. I've already done it."

"My girlfriend found your little website and blog. Paranormal investigator? Come on, man."

Trevor scoffed. "You wouldn't understand. I need this. After everything that happened, this is the only way I can… get around it."

Jake could not believe what he was hearing. "No. No it isn't! Look at me. I've moved on and I did it by forgetting and putting it in the past."

"Well good for you!" Trevor roared, his anger flashing quick and hot. Jake took a step back. He had never known Trevor to get angry, even when they were kids. "I'm not you! I can't just bottle it up and forget about it. I tried, and it almost killed me. Linda was the only thing that saved me. No, the only way I can get through this is closure. Besides, I'm willing to bet you haven't been able to totally block it out."

Jake ground his teeth. The recent episode of Kelly finding the family photo flashed into his memory, and his reaction. He forced it away before Trevor could realize he'd struck a nerve.

"Does Linda know why you are here?" Jake asked.

Trevor did not answer. And when he didn't, Jake knew the truth. And that made him angrier than ever. "Are you serious?" He took long strides toward his brother and got in his face. He'd always been a head taller than him, and now he was wider and weighed more, but Jake did not care. "Trevor, seriously? You can't move your family into this house. You know what lives in there and what it is capable of."

"I'm not a child anymore," Trevor said, not backing away. "I know more about the paranormal than I did then. I can take it on."

"Why would you even try? Why would you put your family in danger for this? It's so stupid."

"Linda and Daniel aren't at risk. I will get rid of this thing once and for all. I'll bring peace to Rose Grove and I'll live the rest of my life knowing I won."

Jake took a step back. He looked his brother up and down — the strong resolve, the cocksure tone of voice, the hard glare. "I won't let you do this. Wreck your life if you want, but Linda's? And *Daniel*?"

"You can't stop me, and you can't tell me what to do," Trevor said. "And if you don't leave I'm calling the police for trespassing."

"I'm not leaving," Jake said. "If you're going to be stupid, then I will stay right here with you and make sure you don't wreck your family like ours."

"You're not staying," Trevor shot back. "I mean it. Get out. You are not welcome here."

Jake almost felt silly. Two brothers arguing as if they were still kids.

He heard the soft squeak of the screen door and Linda poked her head out. "Everything all right, boys?"

"Linda!" Jake said, forcing a smile and adopting a happy tone of voice. He walked up the porch and extended his hand. Linda seemed all too eager to shake it with a bright smile on her face. "My name is Jake Nolan. Trevor's brother. I don't think we have ever been properly introduced." She was a short woman, round body, and cropped red hair that reached the nape of her neck.

"We haven't," she said, casting Trevor a stern look. Trevor watched the two with a scowl. "It's so good to finally meet you."

The next line traditionally should have been *"I've heard so much about you."* But it wasn't true. Jake knew Trevor talked about him less than he told Kelly about Trevor.

"Yeah, well, this has been nice and all," Trevor said, "but Jake was just leaving."

"No way," Linda said, aghast. "You came all this way. You can't just turn around and go. At least stay for dinner."

"He has places to be. Things to do," Trevor said.

"No," Linda said, turning to him and putting a hand on her hip. "We will not send away family at this home." Then, she turned to Jake and softened. "Unless, of course, you really do have plans."

"I think staying for dinner would be nice," Jake said with a smile.

"Then it's settled. Please, come in."

Jake cast a glance to his brother, who glowered at him. Jake was willing to play dirty if he had to.

But when Jake turned to follow Linda, he hesitated. He felt a very strong negative emotion about going back inside his childhood home, and he wondered just what he had gotten himself into. He stared through the window, the foyer familiar yet different. The door was a portal into a hell he wanted nothing to do with.

He heard Trevor approach. "I thought you put it all behind you." Taunting him.

"You can't tell me you didn't freak out the first time you came back," Jake said.

"Of course I did. But I'm here to deal with the problem, not stir up the past, like you." Trevor grabbed him hard by the shoulder and spun him to face him. He got real close, his voice very low and threatening, almost a growl. "You can play on my wife's good graces all you want, but I need you to understand that there is no place here for you. There never will be. As soon as the pleasantries are done, you're gone."

"Fine." Jake met his gaze and did not back down. They stood off for a few tense seconds before the two of them went inside.

9

As soon as Jake set foot into the foyer, he sensed the overwhelming weight of the past come back to him. He remembered that front door, the one he'd passed through so many times. Also those stairs up to the second story with the creaky third step. To the left was the living room with the furniture laid out the same way as it had been when he was a boy. The couch was against the rear wall and faced the television. The fireplace was on the far side. A thick rug covered the hardwood floor.

To the right was the kitchen and dining room. There was not much there because it appeared that was where they were currently remodeling. A ladder stood in the center, surrounded by a clear tarp and paint buckets. Strewn about were hammers, power tools, and nails. It looked like a storm had blown through a workshop, and Jake wondered how Trevor had learned nothing from their father. He had been meticulous about clearing up the equipment at the end of each day, packing them away in case the boys got careless or curious.

"I apologize for the mess," Linda said, looking anguished at the state of her home. "Trev sure is taking his time with the remodeling. Maybe you can help convince him to hire a company that knows what they're doing." She rolled her eyes toward her husband.

"I understand completely," Jake said. "We did the same thing when we were here, and Dad wanted to do it all himself."

"Your father was more of a handyman. No one has lived here since your family. No wonder it was in such disrepair."

"Has it not been owned? Interesting."

Jake cast his brother a look. Trevor frowned. He had not mentioned that. Of course no one had owned the house. That was telling. Everyone was probably scared away by the subtle feeling they got as soon as the real estate agent brought them in.

"All I have is leftover meatloaf," Linda said. "We were not expecting company."

"It sounds wonderful."

"You two boys get comfortable. Don't worry about a thing. I'll prepare dinner."

Jake wandered into the living room, looking around. The room seemed finished. The walls, which had been repainted white when he was young, were now a shade of forest green. He knew Kelly would've hated it, but to each their own. It still smelled of fresh paint and finish and honestly looked quite nice. He couldn't imagine Trevor doing the whole job himself.

But the homeliness was masked by the feeling Jake had

deep within his gut when he walked through the living room. Memories flooded back to him with every new step he took as if each one was a ghost in and of itself that haunted him. The past he had worked so hard to bury was rising up and claiming him again.

He could almost see Dad on the couch, beer in hand, staring at the television but not really watching it. Just waiting for one of his sons to do something wrong…

"Do you feel it?" Trevor asked.

He turned around. For the first time, his brother had spoken to him as if he were a normal human and not a disgusting insect. Instead, he looked concerned, inquisitive.

"Of course. Don't you?"

"Yes. Every day and every night."

"Can they?" Jake nodded toward the kitchen.

"If so, they haven't mentioned it."

"It's still here," Jake said.

"Very much."

"Has anything happened?"

Trevor shook his head. "No. Not yet."

"Then maybe…"

"No. It is definitely here. Probably just waiting. Waiting for the right time to strike. Or something."

Jake was glad their shared experiences in the house could melt away the initial animosity. At once, as soon as stepping inside, the two of them had a common enemy, one that had inflicted far more damage to them than they had ever done to each other.

"Trevor, weird things happened when I decided to come here," Jake said.

"What do you mean?"

"As soon as I booked my flight, a cockroach appeared out of nowhere in the apartment and then disappeared. Do you remember the cockroaches?"

Trevor went white. He didn't answer.

"Do you?" he asked again. Because when it came to those days, Jake could never be sure what Trevor actually remembered.

"Yes, of course I remember the cockroaches," Trevor finally said.

"And on the plane. I heard the voice. It spoke through the headset and broke my screen. It told me not to come."

"Was is the same voice?" Trevor asked. Now he seemed truly interested.

"I'll never forget it. And when I was driving the rental car, I saw a phantom motorcycle. It drove right through me and disappeared. It was trying to run me off the road. Whatever is here knew I was coming, and it didn't want me to arrive." Trevor stroked his narrow goatee as he considered it all. "What have you been doing since you moved in?" Jake asked. "You know… to get rid of it?"

Trevor didn't answer at first, but then he sighed. "A lot of stuff."

"And?"

"And… nothing."

Jake frowned. "What do you mean nothing?"

"Nothing out of the ordinary has happened. No levitations, no apparitions, no personal belongings disappearing and reappearing out of place. All that crap that happened back then… none of it."

Jake knew that was very strange. The skeptic would say there was no ghost in the house anymore, but the heavy, dreadful feeling in Jake's heart told him that wasn't true.

"I even brought in Roger and Keith," Trevor said. "The two other guys in Spirit Seekers, our paranormal investigation group. We spent many nights trying to capture any evidence, but nothing. They won't come back now. They say it's a waste of time."

Footsteps down the stairs made Jake jump — there was almost a PTSD associated with the sound. He remembered it well and how they'd happen in the middle of the night when no one was there. Dad had assumed it was them, and was irate about being woken up at that hour. He'd punished them both very hard for that.

But this time it was only Daniel, who appeared around the corner and stopped short at the edge of the living room, frozen in place by the sudden sight of the stranger in his house.

"Daniel, this is my brother," Trevor told him. "Your uncle Jake."

Daniel, obviously a well-behaved young man, walked up to him and held out his hand. Jake shook it. "Nice to finally meet you."

"You too," Daniel said, his voice high and soft.

"Dinner's ready!" Linda called from the kitchen. Daniel turned around and left him and Trevor alone in the living room again.

"If there's one thing I've learned about the paranormal," Trevor said, "is that changing the environment triggers changes in their behavior. I couldn't pick up anything, but if you're here, maybe it will stir something. Two of its past victims back under the same roof. How could it resist?"

Jake swallowed.

When they were children, Trevor often had no recollection of being attacked by the entity, but Jake figured he'd remember enough to not want to invite the paranormal activity again.

Apparently not.

And now it seemed he planned to use Jake as bait.

10

Due to the renovations, the only piece of furniture in the dining room was a small table. As they ate, they were surrounded by tarps, tools, paint cans, and a giant ladder. Even the light fixture above was a simple light bulb dangling from a wire.

"Again, I'm sorry for this," Linda said for the fourth time. "It's a work in progress. I promise we don't live like this."

"I understand," Jake said, although it did little to assure her. "We lived the same way when we were here."

The meatloaf was great, but the conversation was difficult. Linda did most of the talking, asking Jake questions about where he worked, what he'd been up to the last few years, where he met Kelly, and the rest of the basics.

Trevor and Daniel listened but said nothing. Jake noticed that Linda was careful not to ask anything regarding his and Trevor's past relationship. That meant Trevor had been guarded with her about what had happened to them, not telling her the full story. Just as Jake had been with Kelly.

"Will you be staying with us tonight?" Linda asked.

At that point, Trevor looked up and set his fork down. "I can recommend a good hotel nearby."

"Don't be silly," Linda told him. "We have plenty of space here. The spare room didn't need much work, so it's been completely redone. That was my little contribution to the renovations."

"He can't stay in the spare room," Trevor said. "There are still some problems with the pipes in the walls."

Linda waved her hand. "Psh. The pipes won't matter. Better a room with odd pipes that no one can see or hear than to send your own brother to a hotel. Jake, you are free to stay with us if you want."

"Thank you. I think I will take you up on that offer." He didn't look at Trevor, but he could feel his eyes boring into him.

"Good. Then it's settled."

After dinner, Linda cleared away all the dishes and started cleaning. She sent the men into the living room and told them to relax. The three obeyed, but all they did was zone out and watch television. The news was on, but Jake only half listened to it. Instead, he took out his phone and texted Kelly, telling her that everything was all right and he would stay at the house with his brother. No other details. Not yet. She replied that she was happy that things were going well and to please keep her updated.

Thirty minutes later, Trevor abruptly said, "Daniel, it's time for bed." The boy immediately slid off the seat and walked toward the stairs. "Tell your mother goodnight." Daniel redirected his course to the kitchen where Jake heard the water turn off and Daniel tell Linda he was off to bed. There was a quick kiss and the water resumed. Then he went upstairs.

"Good kid," Jake said. "Very obedient."

"Yeah. He is."

Jake and Trevor had both been mostly behaved when they were young although they got up to some mischief along the way. Usually they were caught and that would mean severe beatings from Dad.

"You should head to bed, too," Trevor said.

"Think I'll stay and see what you do in the middle of the night."

Trevor groaned. Neither of them took their eyes from the television as they spoke. "You're going to get in the way."

"I thought you needed me to make it come out of hiding?"

Linda was the next to go to sleep. Jake and Trevor stayed up with the television on, but neither were paying attention. Instead, they were waiting.

An hour after Linda headed up, Trevor uncrossed his legs and stood from the couch. He walked heavily out of the living room, his weight causing the old floorboards to creak as he went along. Jake heard him rustling around in the closet he remembered was underneath the stairs. When Trevor returned, he dropped a heavy box on to the ground. The cardboard was ripped and falling apart and the side was labeled "Magazines."

But when Trevor opened the flaps, Jake saw it was filled with electronic equipment — a recorder, a microphone, a computer, memory cards, cables, and a camera.

"What's all this?" Jake asked.

"My gear."

"Yeah, I see that. But for what?"

Trevor shot him a look. "For my investigations."

"For ghost hunting?"

"Don't be a smart ass."

Trevor straightened, holding the microphone attached to the recorder. Then, he switched off the television and turned out the light. Night had long since fallen, so the entire room was almost completely dark, silent, and still.

"This is for picking up electronic voice phenomenon," Trevor said. "Basically we record and try to hear the spirit talking to us."

Jake was vaguely familiar with the concept. "How often have you been doing this?" he pressed.

"For three weeks."

"And nothing at all?"

"No."

"So why do you keep trying?"

"Because I know that it is here. And if I continue going with it, eventually I will pick up something."

Jake felt ridiculous standing in the dark, talking to his brother when he couldn't even see his face. But apparently, ghosts preferred the lights out.

Trevor flipped on the recorder and a green light shone. Then he spoke to no one. "Is anyone here?"

He walked around the house, one step at a time at a slow and steady pace to make as little noise as possible. "We want to communicate with you."

Jake watched as his brother went throughout the living room, the foyer, and the kitchen. He wondered how he didn't step on a nail or bump into a ladder in the dark.

"We are not here to hurt you or scare you. We want to help you. But to do that, we need to talk to you first."

Jake had no desire to help the thing that had haunted his childhood, and he knew Trevor felt the same way. So why was he insisting on helping it? Surely if it could send phantom motorcycles after him, it would also know when it was being lied to.

"My brother is here," Trevor said. "You remember us. Is there anything you would like to say?"

Jake's insides twisted as his brother ambled throughout the house, recording the thin air and speaking to something that no one could see. His palms grew sweaty and he could hear his heart beating between his ears. *Why invite that thing? This is so stupid.*

After about an hour, Trevor turned the light back on and the two of them sat on the couch. Trevor took the computer from the box and plugged the recorder into it and downloaded the audio file.

"After every night, I load the footage here and listen," he explained. "I will eventually get something from the other side trying to talk."

When the audio finished transferring, Trevor saved it with the day's date, and played it.

The two of them leaned in, listening closely. Jake heard nothing but silence. The only other sounds were Trevor's questions and requests that the ghost speak, and the heavy footsteps as Trevor tracked around the house.

The screen showed the audio line. It spiked and moved when Trevor spoke, but other than that, it remained straight.

There was no evidence that anything had spoken to him.

Trevor turned the computer off and sighed. "It's been like this for three weeks. Since I first tried on my own after Roger and Keith bailed."

"Are you sure you're doing it right?"

"Of course I am," Trevor said.

The box was full of memory cards, all containing audio from the previous investigations. Trevor leaned back on the couch and rubbed his face. "It won't talk, but it was so interested in telling us it was here when we were young. I can feel it every time I walk inside the house, but it won't budge. I don't understand why."

"Maybe it doesn't want to be found and you should just leave it alone."

Trevor looked at him. "You know I can't do that."

For a moment, Jake took comfort in the fact that the ghost was not responding to Trevor. But how long would that last? It had been very active when they were young, and they had not even tried to talk to it then. Why was it silent now? It definitely wasn't gone. Jake felt the heavy energy all throughout his body, like an invisible, crushing weight. It surely heard Trevor and knew he wanted to communicate.

It's probably waiting for the perfect time to return.

11

Jake lay awake on his back that night, unable to sleep.

The guest bedroom was once Dad's office. The law had been to never, ever, under any circumstances, enter, so sleeping there marked one of the first times Jake had been inside the room. Even years later, he still felt he was breaking a rule.

He couldn't get the image of his brother walking around the house out of his mind. He looked like a crazy person. And honestly, Jake considered it a miracle that nothing had happened.

He's inviting trouble.

Soon after Jake dozed off, he awoke sharply, getting the sudden impression he was not alone in the room. He shot up in bed. "Trevor?"

But no one was there. At least, no one he could see. But he had the unshakable feeling that someone was watching him.

It's lurking. Toying with us.

Jake wondered how long that would be the case before the paranormal activity began again.

He decided that the next day, he would speak with Linda. Find out what she knew and how much she was involved. If Jake could not convince his brother to give up this madness, maybe she could.

MORNING CAME and Jake had not slept. He heard Trevor and Linda walking around upstairs, Daniel getting ready for school, and then Trevor and Daniel leaving. Jake remained in the guest bedroom during all of this, not wanting to interfere with their routine.

He found Linda downstairs, washing up.

"Oh," she said when she saw him, giving him a big smile. "Good morning. How did you sleep?"

"Very well," he lied. "The room was comfortable." That was true enough.

"It's not much, so I apologize. Renovations and all." Linda wiped her hands on a dishtowel. "Can I make you some breakfast? Eggs and toast?"

"Oh. No, thank you."

"You have to eat." She smiled.

"Yeah, but… I've already put you out."

"You're not putting me out. Now that Trev and Daniel are gone, I was going to prepare breakfast for myself."

Jake's stomach rumbled. "I suppose. But only if you were doing it anyway…"

Without another word, Linda set to work on cooking. Jake retrieved his laptop from upstairs and checked his email. He had a message from his boss.

. . .

Hey Jake, hope everything is well. Client emails are still being forwarded to you, but if you need time away, I understand. Let me know how to proceed forward.

Jake was glad he understood. He wondered how much good grace he would get from him until it dried up.

There was no way he could tell him the family emergency was his brother moving into a haunted house.

Jake's main clients for his graphic design company he worked for had mostly given him projects for logos. He thought it funny how most new companies prioritized a good logo before they got anything else off the ground.

Still, they were paying customers, and he was happy to oblige.

He couldn't even go through all his messages before Linda called for him.

They sat at the dining room table. Jake had a plate of fried eggs and links of sausage. Linda had the same, and in between them, a basket of toast with butter and jam.

"Smells amazing," Jake said, sitting down.

"Can whip it up in five minutes."

As Linda chewed, she cast her eyes around — at the tarp, the paint, the brushes, and the general mess that surrounded her. Her lip curled.

Jake cleared his throat. "Not a fan of the renovations?" he asked.

"Just ready for it to be done."

"The living room looks nice."

"Trev started there because there wasn't much to do.

But now the progress has slowed. It's almost as if he's losing interest and he won't hire anyone. He can be stubborn sometimes."

"Tell me about it," Jake said, rolling his eyes.

"Maybe you can help convince him to hire a company," Linda said. "Yeah, it costs more, but it'd be so nice to stop living in this chaos."

"In case you haven't noticed, he doesn't care about what I have to say."

Linda set down her fork and wiped her mouth with a napkin. "What happened between the two of you? If you don't mind me asking."

Jake scratched at his chin. His stubble had grown. "So he hasn't told you much about the past."

"Not at all," Linda said. "I heard this house is supposed to be haunted, but —" she shrugged. "I haven't seen anything. And neither has he."

Jake didn't answer. If she was a skeptic that was fine. But he knew the truth.

And then she started to cry.

At first her face scrunched up, and when she realized she would not be able to keep it in, she let the sobs go and the tears welled up.

"Oh," Jake said awkwardly. "What…"

She shook her head. "Sorry." She used her napkin to dab her eyes and wipe her nose. "It's just…"

Jake didn't know what to do, so he sat there and allowed her have her a moment.

When she got her sobs under control, she said, "If he wants to join this group and run around chasing ghosts, that's fine. Everyone needs a hobby and Roger and Keith are great guys. But this is different. To move us into this house and spend all your time trying to talk to spirits or make them appear or whatever... I mean, come on, the water in the downstairs bathroom doesn't even work right now! What are the priorities?"

"If it helps, I also think he's crazy for coming here because of a ghost." Although Jake had very different reasons for feeling that way.

"It's not about that," Linda said. "Trevor's... changed. I realize you haven't spoken to him in a long time, but it's true. He is not the man he once was."

"How so?"

"He's just... unusual. He's very prone to quick changes in mood. Like remember yesterday? He was angry when he saw you, but later he was civil? Perfect example."

Jake had indeed noted his brother's sharp change in hostility as the evening had worn on.

"Him and Daniel used to be inseparable," Linda said. "Now he sends him off to his room early so he has more time to play with his recorders and videos and other toys." She pushed her plate away. "And don't think about suggesting there isn't a ghost here. Oh no. He's fine if I'm a skeptic about his other paranormal projects, but with this house, no way. You should've heard the fights we've had over the ghost that's supposed to live here. It's almost like he needs that thing to exist."

It's happening again, Jake thought. *Tearing apart the family that lives here.*

"Anyway," Linda said. "I'm sorry. I don't know what came over me. I guess I had to get all that off my chest. Maybe you can talk some sense into him. Unless you also believe there's a ghost inside this house."

"I'll see what I can do," Jake said, frowning.

The entity did not even have to appear to cause discord.

Linda stood and cleared her and Jake's plates without asking if he was done. Jake let his half-eaten breakfast go.

As she washed up, Jake spotted a pile of paint cans, old brushes, and peeled off painters tape in the corner of the dining room — trash Trevor hadn't yet bothered to discard.

"Linda," Jake said, walking into the kitchen. "I'll take those empty cans out to the end of the driveway so recycling can pick them up."

"Jake, you don't have to do that," Linda said.

"I want to. My brother won't do it so maybe I'll help get him started."

Linda gave a small smile. "Well. If it gives him a hint, then why not?"

So he set to work stacking the paint cans and other trash. But as he worked, he noticed something under the garbage that did not belong.

A wooden crucifix.

He picked it out of the pile and examined it, wondering why it was there. *Odd thing to toss out like this...*

"Linda?" Jake called.

"Yeah?"

"Is there a reason this is being thrown away?"

Linda peeked around the corner from the kitchen. When she saw what he had, her eyes widened. "Oh my goodness!" Dishes forgotten, she rushed over to him and snatched the crucifix from his hands as if he were threatening to break it. "I've been searching for this for weeks! Where did you find it?"

"In that pile."

Linda froze. "No way. What was it doing under there?"

Jake shrugged. "I swear. I moved a few paint cans, and it was underneath them."

She furrowed her brow. "That doesn't make sense. This was my mother's, and I thought we'd lost it in the move." She placed it gently on the dining room table. "Trevor's going to catch hell for dropping it in his mess. He knows how much this means to me."

She returned to the kitchen. Jake stared at the object, knowing the answer wasn't as simple as that.

Trevor wouldn't just lose that thing in the trash.

Then, right before his eyes, the crucifix flew from the table at blinding speed and crashed into the stack of paint cans, sending them tumbling and rolling and clanging on the floor.

Linda poked her head around the corner again. "Jake? What was that? Are you all right?"

"Yeah," Jake said. "Knocked over the cans by accident. No problem."

The crucifix lay among the mess, hurled by unseen hands back into the trash.

And a heavy knot formed in the pit of Jake's stomach.

12

1995

Summer was half over.

Jason came to invite Jake and Trevor out to play every day, but Jake always turned him down after Trevor showed no interest. Eventually, Jason quit stopping by. So did Brian, and Peter, and all the rest.

One morning, Jake and Trevor sat watching cartoons, and Jake realized it was the third time they'd seen that episode in past couple weeks. Mom and Dad were arguing on the landing upstairs, which was becoming more frequent than the rerun currently on the screen.

"I knew the joint was run down, but the real estate guy didn't mention all this shit in the sidewall," Dad shouted from the upstairs landing. "The whole thing practically needs to be redone!" A loud smack landed on the wall.

"Harry, why are you screaming? You never used to talk to me like this." Mom sounded on the verge of tears.

"I'm not talking to you, I'm talking to the sidewall!"

"Can you just hire someone?"

"And spend even more money? Did you seriously just say that to me?"

"But the whole project has already —" Mom trailed off, and even Jake winced as he predicted what was coming. Even he knew not to question Dad's handyman skills.

"Yeah, you'd better shut your mouth before you say the wrong thing."

Heavy footsteps boomed as Dad came downstairs, then turned into the living room. He fixed them in his dark gaze and Jake sank back into the cushion.

"What's going on here?" Dad said. "It's summer and you two just sit in here watching TV all day."

Trevor held up his casted arm in response.

"You broke your arm, Trev, but you're acting like you're decapitated. Get the hell off my couch and go outside and play."

Once outside, Dad slammed the door behind them. Jake thought he even heard it lock.

Although he didn't like being yelled at by Dad, especially when they didn't do anything wrong, Jake figured this was a good start in getting Trevor back to his old self. "Do you want to go to the park and see if Jason and them are there?"

Trevor didn't answer. He only sat on the porch step and leaned his head against the wooden railing.

Jake went and sat next to his brother. "What's going on? Dad's right. All you did was break your arm, but you're acting way weirder."

"I just don't feel like it, okay?" Trevor said, words terse and impatient.

"Why? What's going on?"

Trevor stood and stomped off away from him.

And Jake knew there was something else going on with this brother. Affecting him more than his broken arm. And he wished he could figure out what it was.

ONE NIGHT IN LATE JULY, Jake woke up in the middle of the night. He had been dreaming of the black form again. What he had seen in the tree house made reoccurring visits in his nightmares. Sometimes it just stood there. Other times it took the shape of a person or an animal — even ones he wasn't sure existed. But always, in all the dreams Jake could tell that it hated him, wanted to hurt him. Waking up was a welcome relief.

So when he woke up, he rolled over. And almost leapt out of bed in fright.

At first he thought it was the black shadow again, but then his sense took over and saw what it really was — his brother, standing near the door.

"Trevor?" Jake whispered. He did not answer. "Trevor!"

Still nothing.

Jake leaned over and switched on the lamp on the table between their two beds. His brother stood in his pajamas, his back facing him, staring at the wall.

"Hey, Trev. What are you doing?"

No response. It was like he hadn't heard him at all.

Jake threw off the covers and went to his brother, standing only a few inches away. He tapped his shoulder.

Trevor did not turn around. His eyes were open, face calm and still, hair disheveled from sleep. Though Jake was right in front of him, his brother could not even see him.

Sleepwalking.

Which was very weird. Jake had never known Trevor to sleepwalk before.

He remembered from somewhere that he was not supposed to wake a sleepwalker. But this was his brother, and he was scaring him. He had been acting strange for so long — ever since he broke his arm — and now this was the strangest thing of all.

Jake tried to shake him awake. "Trevor, wake up." His body jiggled under his grasp, but he felt rigid, as if every muscle was tense and unable to move.

Then, Trevor started to walk. Slowly and deliberately, one foot after the other. He opened the bedroom door and walked into the upstairs hallway.

"Trevor!" Jake whispered as loud as he could. His brother still did not hear him.

Jake's heart thudded as he debated what to do. If Dad caught them out of bed, they would be in huge trouble. He didn't like it when they stayed up late, and he liked it even less when they disobeyed him. And bedtime was one of his biggest rules.

Trevor walked down the hallway and turned, descending the stairs, and soon was out of sight.

"Where are you going?" Jake whispered after him.

The sound of Trevor's footsteps faded as he got further away. Jake remained at the threshold of the door, standing his ground, afraid to step over the line as if it were some kind of invisible barrier that would vaporize him if he crossed. With his father's temper, it might as well be.

In the distance, Jake heard the front door open and close.

What are you doing?

Jake remained in the bedroom, deciding to wait until his brother came back. He did not want to go after him and risk making too much noise and wake up their father. That would only make things worse.

So Jake sat in bed and waited for what felt like hours. The house was silent and there was no sign of Trevor returning.

Then, out of the corner of his eye, he saw movement through the bedroom window.

Although it was so dark, he recognized the unmistakable outline of Trevor at the base of the tree. His brother's back was to him, and he stared up into the branches.

"Trevor," Jake said. He beat on the glass as loud as he dared. His dad was a notoriously light sleeper.

But Trevor did not hear.

Instead, he climbed the ladder.

Jake froze as he watched, amazed. His brother climbed as if nothing was wrong with his arm. He maneuvered it around as if the cast were not there. Very strange, as Trevor had been using his arm as an excuse to sit around all summer.

But not that night. He shot up the tree fast and sure, like an animal returning to its nest.

In a few seconds he was on top of the thick branch that led to the tree house.

Jake tried to bang on the window again. If his brother were sleepwalking, then any wrong step would send him tumbling out of the tree. If that were to happen, Trevor would have far more than only a broken arm.

Trevor walked down the branch as if he were walking down the hallway of his own house. His feet landed sure and confident and he never stumbled. He disappeared inside the dark tree house and Jake no longer saw him.

Jake knew that thing was in the tree house. Knew that shadow was the reason Trevor was going up there.

But why?

Jake watched for a long time, waiting for something to happen. Anything. He hoped his brother would come back, but he didn't.

A light turned on inside the tree house. One of the old flashlights they had left up there that first night. The same flashlight that had not worked for Jake when he had gone to get the comic books.

Trevor was a dark silhouette against the tree house window. He stood directly in the center, and Jake was not sure if he was looking at him or facing away.

Jake tried tapping on the window again, this time knocking it so loud the glass rattled in the pane. He unlocked it and pushed it open. "Trevor!"

But his brother was completely unmoving inside the tree house. Unnaturally still.

Jake knew he had to get him. This had gone too far, and they were for sure going to be caught if he didn't make a move.

Jake went downstairs and crept out the front door, then around the house and to the base of the tree. When he got there, the flashlight was still on at the top.

"Trevor!" he tried calling one last time, and when there was no response, he climbed.

He rose nervously, like the other two times. But he kept his fear at bay — he was doing this for his brother.

But then, when he was halfway up the tree, he could not climb anymore.

Not because he was afraid, but because he was physically unable. It felt as if some unseen wall was blocking his path. As if gravity in that one section of the earth was three times stronger than normal.

Jake tried to push through it, knowing whatever lived in their tree house was trying to keep him from getting to his brother.

Then he pushed too hard. A strong, invisible force flung him off the ladder. He fell and landed on his back on the grass, banging his head on the ground, seeing stars.

"*Jake!*"

He sat up and turned to see his father storming across the backyard. He had that forceful walk he did when he was furious. "What the hell are you doing out here so late at night!"

Jake curled into a ball and tears filled his eyes. He knew what was coming next. But first he had to tell the truth. "It's Trevor! I think he's sleepwalking. He's going to hurt himself."

"Trevor? Where?"

Jake pointed up to the tree house. When Dad looked up, he grew even angrier.

"Trevor! Get your ass down here right now."

Trevor did not hear.

"I'm counting to three! If you're not down here before then, you'll be sorry."

Dad slowly started to count. Jake already knew that tactic. It had inspired fear in them their entire lives and, for the first time, it'd be unsuccessful that night.

In the end, Dad had to climb up to the tree house

himself to get Trevor. Jake heard him shout and smack Trevor, and Trevor screamed and cried.

"I told you to come down! What do you think you're doing?"

"I'm sorry," Trevor pleaded beneath his cries. "I don't know what I'm doing up here!"

Trevor had no memory of going up there. Jake also knew his father would never believe either of them. To him, this could only be a case of deliberate disobedience that would be punished harshly.

And it was.

Both Jake and Trevor were bruised for weeks.

13

1995

Jake stood in front of the mirror, his back to it and his head twisted around as best he could, straining to see over his shoulder. His shorts were pulled down to his thigh, exposing his bottom. It was covered with purple and yellow bruises that wouldn't go away anytime soon. He lifted his shirt and inspected the marks on his back as well. They ended halfway up the back.

It was the most savage spanking he'd ever experienced. Dad had spanked him before, both him and Trevor, whenever they got up to mischief, but nothing as fierce as this one. Jake knew he would never forget it.

He was thrown over Dad's leg, pants yanked down, and slapped hard, over and over, the pain shooting and jolting through his entire body. His father seemed to lose control, not even bothering to aim anymore, which resulted in the slaps landing on his back as well. He had gone off on him completely, just wanting to hurt him.

If Mom had been around, she would have pulled him off.

Trevor got the same treatment. It did not matter that he had a broken arm.

They were sent to bed and told to go to sleep. But sleep would be impossible after what had happened.

The two sobbed in their beds. They instinctively knew they had a limited amount of time when crying was accepted, and that eventually Dad would come in and tell them to shut up with all that blubbering. He might even beat them again.

So they forced themselves into silence, tears leaking out of their eyes.

Until finally Trevor whispered. "Why did he do that?"

Jake looked over to his brother, but had a hard time seeing him in the darkness. "What do you mean?"

"Why did Dad hit us like that?"

Jake could not believe what he was hearing. "Because you climbed into the tree house in the middle of the night. And I went out to get you down, but you weren't listening to me. Why were you ignoring me?"

Trevor said nothing for a long time. "I didn't go to the tree house."

"Yes you did," Jake said. "I saw it with my own eyes."

"No. I didn't."

Jake propped himself on this elbow, looking at his brother in the dark. "You mean you don't remember climbing the tree?"

"Why would I do that? I can't climb it with my arm."

"You did. I watched you do it. You shot up quick like your arm wasn't even broken. Then you walked on the branch like you weren't afraid you would fall. You went inside the tree house and just stood there for a long time."

"Really?" Trevor's voice trailed off. "I don't remember any of that."

"I swear it's true. I thought you were sleepwalking."

Trevor rolled over in bed, putting his back to him. "I would never go into the tree house after falling. I don't think that happened."

Jake knew there was no way to convince his brother of what he saw, nor Dad that Trevor had been sleepwalking. Dad would not listen — he assumed everything was deliberate disobedience. But Jake was sure of what he had seen.

JAKE COULD NOT SIT down for a week without pain. Trevor was the same. Mom gave them pitying looks, but said nothing. She rarely came between Dad and his discipline.

Every night, after they went to bed, Jake felt an obligation to stay awake to keep a watchful eye on his brother. Just in case it happened again. He even fell into the habit of sleeping in front of the bedroom door so he could be kicked awake if Trevor tried to get out.

Then, one week later, Jake was awake in the middle of the night, reading with a flashlight while standing guard when Trevor got out of bed.

He moved in the same dreamlike trance as he had before, standing still at first, and then heading toward the door. He reached for the doorknob but found it locked. Jake had started locking the bedroom door at night, just in case.

Jake stood and blocked his brother's path to the door. In his trance, he persisted in trying to press on, but Jake only lightly pushed him back. "Trevor," he whispered, trying to get his brother's attention, but he heard nothing.

Jake knew he was trying to go back to the tree house. Whatever was in that tree — that thing — was doing this. It was not sleepwalking. It was taking over Trevor's body and making him do things he wouldn't normally do. Things *it* wanted him to do.

After an hour of blocking him, Trevor returned to his bed and went back to sleep.

The next morning, Jake asked him, "Do you remember anything from last night?"

"No," Trevor said. "Why? Did something happen?"

"Forget it."

And Trevor left it at that. As if he did not want to know.

Jake knew he needed help. Without it, these things would continue happening. And, if he accidentally fell asleep while on watch and Trevor got out, there would be no stopping him.

He couldn't tell any of his friends. The neighborhood boys had stopped coming around since his self-imposed reclusion with his injured brother. Besides, they would only laugh at him if he told them about the ghost that lived in his tree house.

He couldn't tell Mom because she would not believe him. Dad might not either, but he could at least think up a solution. Maybe he would lock all the doors in the house. Or let Trevor sleep in their room for a while so they could see the trance for themselves.

It might work, Jake told himself. After all, Dad was always interested in things that kept his boys on their best behavior.

One evening, after dinner, Dad reclined on the couch in the dark, the only light coming from the glow on the television. He watched a baseball game, the volume turned low.

He stared at the screen, emotionless, as if he were in a trance himself. He sank deep into the worn cushion, a beer can in his hand. His black hair was thick and disheveled and greasy, and the beard on his face was coming in full.

He looked so different, so terrible. It had all started when they had moved into the house.

Jake sauntered into the living room, still not certain of his decision. But there was nowhere else to turn.

"Dad?" He did not respond. Only stared at the television, the light flickering across his face. "Dad?"

Then, he turned and looked at his son. His expression frightened Jake — a look of pure hatred, although he was sure he was imagining it. There was no way his own father hated him, right?

"What?"

"I have something to tell you."

Dad let out a long groan. He did not like to be interrupted when he was watching a game.

"What have you done? Do you need another whipping?"

"No," Jake said quickly. "It's about Trevor."

"You going to tattle on your brother now? Are you sure you didn't do it and you're just trying to pin it on him?"

"No," Jake said. "I didn't do anything wrong. But I'm worried about Trevor."

"What about him?"

"He… acts weird at night."

"Acts weird how?"

Jake now had his father's full attention. "He… sleep-walks. He gets up and walks around and tries to leave the room, but I lock the door so he can't. I think he's trying to go to the tree house again."

"Both you and Trevor know not to go into the tree house at night anymore. Or do I need to remind you?"

"No!" Jake said, desperate. This was not going how he planned, so perhaps it was time to get to the point. "The night that Trevor broke his arm. I don't think he fell. He was pushed."

Dad stared at him. He leaned forward and set the can the floor between his feet. Their faces were close and Jake smelled the beer on his breath. Saw the lines and wrinkles in his face that had not been there a few short months ago.

"Go on," his father said, voice low.

"I saw it. I was sitting in the tree house and he was on the branch. He didn't lose his balance. But the way he fell looked like someone had pushed him." Jake now realized it was hard to explain, and he felt stupid.

"If that's true, then why did Trevor say he fell?"

"Because he didn't know he was pushed."

"Is this your way of telling me you threw your brother out of the tree?" His voice rose.

"No! I swear!"

"Then what are you saying? Someone else did it?"

"Yes."

Dad's brow furrowed. "Do you realize how crazy you sound?"

"But there's more. One night, Trevor asked me to go back to the tree house and get the comic books we left up there. So I went, and I saw something."

"Saw what?"

"It was very dark. Like a shadow. There is something in the tree, and it pushed Trevor. And it makes him walk around at night because Trevor always wants to go to the tree house when he's sleepwalking."

Jake couldn't read the expression on Dad's face. It was a mixture of anger, annoyance, and exhaustion.

"So you're saying, Jake, that there's a ghost that lives in the tree, and this ghost pushed your brother and what causes you two to act like little shits in the middle of the night?"

"Yes."

It was great to have it off his chest, to confess. There was something strange going on and it only affected him and Trevor. And they needed help.

It happened so fast that Jake had no time to prepare. Dad's hand lashed out and caught him against the cheek. The backhanded slap cracked against his skin, sending him stumbling backwards. Jake raised a palm to his face, his eyes watering from the sting. He blinked them back, knowing better than to cry in his father's presence.

"Don't blame a ghost for your bad behavior," Dad said through gritted teeth. "You're a piss poor child and you need more discipline. You expect me to be told by an eight-year-old that there's a ghost that lives in the tree outside? How stupid do you think I am?" Dad's anger rose, and he stood from the couch, towering over him. Jake stepped backwards, trying to put some distance between himself and his father.

"A ghost?" Dad shouted. "A ghost! That is the stupidest thing I've ever heard. How dare you try to pull this one over on me!" He was screaming now, and Jake did the only thing he could think to do — he turned and ran.

He dashed up the stairs, scrambling, hoping his father didn't follow.

He didn't, but his booming voice did.

"Don't you ever say anything like that to me again! You're a stupid little kid if you believe ghosts exist! I never want to hear that shit come out of your mouth again!"

Jake flew into his bedroom and slammed the door behind him, then locked it.

Trevor looked at him from where he sat on the floor, eyes wide with terror.

The two of them stood there in silence, waiting for Dad's tantrum to end. He never came up the stairs, thank God, but he shouted at them from the bottom of the steps. Jake realized then he was drunk, and should have known better than to talk to him when he had a beer in his hand. It was probably his sixth or seventh of the night, having begun when he came home from work.

Finally, Dad fell quiet.

"What happened?" Trevor asked. "Your face is red."

Jake inspected his cheek in the mirror. Trevor was right — it shone. And it stung. It would leave yet another bruise.

And Jake had learned an important lesson. Dad would

not help them. He was silly to think he could, or would. Whatever was going on with this *thing* in the tree, it was up to him and Trevor to handle it themselves.

From that night on, Jake vowed never to mention it to anyone ever again.

14

2018

They had spaghetti for dinner that evening. As they ate, Linda asked Daniel about his day at school, and what he had learned. A science fair was coming up, and that would require a large project. The boy seemed excited to embark on the task and already had an idea — he wanted to do something that involved the planets.

Linda encouraged him. But as she spoke, Trevor remained silent, engaged only with his food. Jake caught Linda throwing him several concerned glances.

"Doesn't that sound good, Trevor?"

"Yeah. Great," he mumbled.

When dinner was over, Jake excused himself to the living room while Linda and Trevor had a hushed argument about his detachment in the kitchen. Daniel went upstairs to do homework.

Trevor returned a few minutes later where he

collapsed on the couch next to Jake and turned on the television. He flipped the channels until he found an old science fiction movie and let the remote drop to his side.

"How was work?" Jake asked.

"Lousy. How was sitting around here?"

"Fine." The sight of the crucifix hurling itself across the room had been with Jake all day, and he waited for the right time to tell Trevor.

They hung out on the couch for a while until Linda came in and announced that she was going to bed. "Please try not to stay up too late. You wake me up when you get under the covers." Her tone was soft and weak, her strength sapped by the emotional morning she'd had. Trevor didn't know the half of it.

"Good night," Trevor said, without even looking at her.

"Sleep well," Jake said, attempting to be more pleasant.

She disappeared upstairs.

Thirty minutes later, Trevor peeled himself off the couch.

"Wait," Jake said, and Trevor stopped. "What are you doing?"

"I'm getting the recording equipment."

"Before you do that, listen. Do you remember that old crucifix that belonged to Linda's grandmother?"

"Yes." He gave him a curious look. "I caught hell because of that thing. Apparently it was in the trash from the renovations. No idea how that happened."

"Come on. You know how it ended up there."

Trevor took a few seconds to process, and then his eyes grew wide. "Of course!"

"Not only that. I put it on the table, and then I watched it fly *by itself* back into the trash pile."

Trevor stared at him for a long time, the implications of what Jake was saying seeping into his brain. He sank back onto the couch. "You're sure? You're not messing with me?"

"I swear," Jake said. "It's the only unexplained thing I've seen since I've been here."

"And the first paranormal activity for me too." Trevor shot up again and left the room.

When he returned, he held the crucifix in his hand. A new excitement filled his eyes. "Linda asked me to hang this above the front door after dinner. Good thing I put it off."

Trevor held the cross in his hands, looking down on it with reverence. "I don't know if you've found God yet, Jake, but if you haven't, I recommend you do some soul searching. Religion was the only thing that has carried me through the last couple years after everything that happened."

Jake was surprised and not surprised at the same time. Their family had never been religious growing up, but he and Trevor had obviously found very different ways of coping with their trauma.

Whatever you need to get through.

"I love this thing," Trevor said. "We hung it above the front door at our last house. I guess I believed it would keep whatever had attacked us from following me to my new home."

"Until you came back looking for it."

His brother looked up at him. "It's the only way I know how to move on."

Trevor held the crucifix out in front of him at arm's

length. He stood there for a few seconds and then spoke. "If you are here, we want to communicate with you."

The lights flickered. Once, twice, three times. Then they went completely dark.

The temperature in the room plunged to freezing. Jake felt as if he had been dunked into an ice bath.

"What the hell?" Jake whispered. He wrapped his arms around his body, trying to warm himself.

The entire house was silent. With the lights off, Jake could not see one foot in front of his eyes. Trevor waited for a while before speaking again. "You've given a sign and we know you are here. Please talk to us."

Trevor let out a yelp, followed by a loud crash to Jake's right. At first, he thought Trevor had been flung, as the crucifix had been earlier. Jake crossed the room and found the light switch. He flicked it up and down a few times before the lights in the living room came back on.

The crucifix was pinned to the wall, upside down.

Jake and Trevor stared in disbelief, then looked at each other.

"So," Trevor said. "It stays silent this whole time. But when I take out the cross, it becomes active."

"It doesn't like it."

Trevor walked over to the upside down cross and inspected it. Nothing was holding it in place — as if it was glued there.

"Don't touch," Jake said.

Trevor didn't listen. He reached out and ran his fingers along the wood, gripped the long part of the cross and pulled, but it didn't budge. He yanked harder until it came off the wall, causing Trevor to stumble backward.

He inspected it. "Still normal."

"We should stop this," Jake said. He had a very uneasy feeling. He briskly rubbed his hands over his arms, trying to warm up.

"Are you serious? We've finally gotten a response."

"Trevor," Jake tried again. "I really think we shouldn't mess around with this thing. You remember what it used to do to us. We can't piss it off."

But Trevor was of a different opinion. Jake saw it in his brother's eyes. He almost looked a little unhinged, desperate, excited to see what would happen next.

Trevor raised the crucifix again. He opened his mouth to speak, but before any words came out, the lights shut off again.

"Trevor!" Jake said.

There was a loud crashing sound again, this time from above.

Trevor jiggled the switch a few times and light filled the room. The crucifix was stuck on the ceiling, just as it had been on the wall.

Cracks in the plaster surrounded the cross, and some bits had crumbled to the hardwood floor at their feet. It had been thrown with a much stronger force than before.

And now neither of them could reach it.

"Unbelievable," Trevor said, looking up, as if witnessing a natural wonder of the world.

"It isn't. We've seen all this before."

"Wait here." Trevor rushed upstairs.

Jake knew it was wrong, that they were playing with fire. This thing — whatever it was — was willing to desecrate a religious symbol, and they definitely should not be messing around.

Trevor returned, wearing a heavy jacket and holding a big Bible. "Had this packed away in the bedroom," he said.

"What are you doing?"

Trevor didn't answer. Instead he held the book up as he'd done with the crucifix. He began to speak, but before he could, an invisible force smacked the Bible from his hand.

The cover opened by itself and the thin pages flipped as if being blown by a strong wind that was not there. The pages flipped again in the other direction, back and forth.

Then they started to rip.

They were torn to shreds on the ground between them. The fragments of the Scriptures floated into the air like confetti. By the time the ghost finished, nothing remained between the covers of the Bible.

"We've found the trigger," Trevor said, amazed.

"We need to stop." Jake shivered and his breath frosted in front of his lips. "This isn't right at all."

"It is exactly what we needed," Trevor said. "Now that we know how to draw it out, we can send it away."

Jake met his brother's gaze, and he felt like he was eye-to-eye with a madman. He couldn't believe what he was hearing.

As if it will not fight back. As if it's going to go quietly.

15

Ripping the Bible was the final word from the spirit that night. When the freezing temperature in the living room returned to normal, Trevor determined that the spirit had gone.

"We'll keep working tomorrow night," he said.

Jake went to bed even though he had no idea how he was going to get any sleep. He lay awake, staring at ceiling in the dark room, wondering what he should do.

It never left. It's been here all this time.

He wondered if it had drawn the two of them back on purpose. Had done some sort of manipulation to get he and his brother under its roof. It had destroyed the other members of their family, and maybe it was not content until it finished the job.

I need help. If Trevor is insisting on doing this, he cannot do it alone.

It was only a matter of time before this thing attacked Linda and Daniel. Jake felt it in his gut.

He rolled over and pulled the covers up to his chin. He

could flee. Pack his bag and drive away, tell himself he tried, and leave Trevor up to his own fate. But he would be abandoning Linda and Daniel too, and they did not deserve to suffer for the stupidity of their father.

Help was the only way. But where would he get it? Who would ever believe him about what was happening in the house?

And in the late hours, a single option came to Jake's mind.

In the morning, Jake went downstairs and peeked into the living room to see if any trace remained of what happened the night before. The torn Bible pages were gone, and the cross had been taken off the ceiling. The ladder from the dining room was now underneath the cracked spot in the plaster. Trevor must have climbed and removed it. That surprised Jake because the entity could have easily pushed him off.

He found Linda in the kitchen preparing breakfast.

"You're just in time," she said when she spotted him.

The two of them sat down at the dining room table the same way they had the previous morning.

"Trevor didn't come to bed until late last night," Linda said as they ate.

"You know how he is," was all Jake said. He did not want to elaborate. Did not want to scare her. She was already going through enough as it was as far as her husband was concerned.

Once breakfast concluded, Linda returned to the kitchen and cleaned up. Jake brought his laptop to the dining room table. Only a single idea for help had come to him and he hoped it was still a viable option.

He searched for someone named Arthur Briggs, a name from his past.

When they were children, their mother eventually realized their house was haunted. Dad, of course, would not hear of it. One day, when he was out, Mom called a man over to investigate. He'd claimed to be a priest and paranormal investigator and that he would help.

But as he was getting started, Dad came home. And he was not happy. It was the first time Jake had ever seen his father physically assault someone besides him and his brother. And for that reason, Jake would never forget his name.

According to the Internet, Arthur Briggs was still alive, and in the area. He owned a simple website that had not been updated in a while, but it talked about his past work as a priest — nothing involving the supernatural. Jake found an email address at the bottom of the site, which he clicked.

Mr. Briggs,

My name is Jake Nolan. I'm sure you don't remember me, but years ago you came to my house in Rose Grove, Georgia. My mother called you because she believed our home was haunted. Now, my brother has purchased the place with the goal of getting rid of the ghost that caused so many problems when we were children. Last night, we finally got the ghost to give us a sign it was still here. It did not like the cross we were holding, and took it from our hands and tried to put it places where we could not reach. Also, it ripped up a Bible right in front of our eyes. I told my brother to contact professional help, but he won't, saying that this is too personal, so that is why I am writing to you. Can you please advise me of what to do in this situation?

HE REREAD the email and found it utterly ridiculous. But it was an exact play-by-play of the night before, so Jake forced himself to send.

He took a deep breath and went to the refrigerator to grab something to drink. The fridge was in the same place as when he was a kid. It had been full of Dad's beer and the toy alphabet magnets that used to litter to the bottom section of the door. Jake shivered when he remembered those magnets and the trouble they caused him and Trevor.

As he returned to his laptop with a can of Coke in hand, something caught his eye in its periphery. In the living room, the ladder was upside down. It balanced on its head, the legs sprawled in the air like a headstand. Jake approached it, staring with wonder.

And in terror.

They had stirred it up last night. It would start again. All those strange occurrences that Dad blamed on him and Trevor, getting them into trouble — and beaten — constantly.

"You've done it now, Trev," Jake whispered.

He pulled the ladder down and put it right side up before Linda saw.

Jake spent the rest of the morning working at the dining room table. He caught up on work emails and applied finishing touches on some logo designs before sending them off to his clients for approval.

Someone knocked on the front door.

Knock-knock-knock.

Was Linda expecting anyone? She was in the back of the house, ironing clothes.

Knock-knock-knock.

"Linda," Jake called.

She came through the kitchen. "Yeah?"

"Are you expecting a visitor?"

"No. Why?"

"Ah. Someone's knocking."

"Oh." She seemed pleasantly surprised to have an unexpected guest.

Linda went to the door and opened it, but then closed it and returned to the dining room. "No one was there. Are you sure you heard something?"

Jake looked up from the computer. He understood.

There was never anyone there.

Knocking was a common strategy the entity used to upset Dad, especially late at night. Jake winced when he remembered how fiercely him and Trevor were punished for the knocking they didn't do.

"Yeah. Maybe just some kids or something," Jake improvised.

"We live far off the main road. I would have seen them running away."

"Maybe I mistook it."

Linda shrugged. "Hey, do you know why the ladder's in the living room? And why the ceiling is cracked? What in the world did Trevor get up to last night after I went to bed?"

"You'll have to ask him," Jake said. Linda grumbled as she returned to the back of the house.

When she left, Jake got up and went to the front door. He opened it and stepped out onto the porch. As Linda said, nothing was there. "Shit," he muttered. It would start in full force. Tormenting them again.

He returned to his computer in time to hear a chime. He'd received a reply from Arthur Briggs.

Mr. Nolan.

Yes, of course I remember you, and the house. That was a long time ago, and you were just a boy, and it was an unfortunate incident that occurred when I was there. I hold no hard feelings toward your father or your family. I understand why he reacted the way he did and I hope they are well.

That being said, I would urge you and your brother to leave the house. If anyone else is living there, take them with you. I will never forget the feeling I had when I walked through that house back then, and if nothing was ever done to cleanse it, then you can bet the spirit is still inside.

Based on what you described, I would say you do not have a ghost. A ghost was once a human that is remaining behind. Sometimes he does not even realize he is dead and needs encouragement to pass on. Many of them don't mean to scare you — they are only trying to communicate.

But your situation is different. The spirit that in that house is inhuman, and never was human. What you have described is a demonic presence. I determined this based on one clue alone — it does not like religious objects. This is a dangerous and blasphemous creature, and its goal is to frighten you and, eventually, harm you.

I apologize for the blunt nature of my message, but you need to know and understand. You must leave the home, and I mean this with all of my heart.

If you require any other help or advice, please do not hesitate to call me.

THE EMAIL ENDED with a signature and a phone number.

Inhuman.

Demonic.

Jake felt the breath leave his body. He looked around the dining room and kitchen and got the strange, shaky feeling that someone was with him. Watching him. But there was nothing that he could see.

Arthur Briggs was right. They needed to get out.

Jake remembered what happened when they were kids. It delighted the entity to get them in trouble with Dad, to frame them for bad behavior they didn't do, and pit the family against each other by doing crazy things they blamed on each other. It had even outright pushed Trevor from the tree when it didn't like them there.

The same process had already begun with Trevor's family. By not responding to Trevor, it caused him to detach from them while he obsessed on making contact, driving a wedge between him and Linda and Daniel.

And now that they'd confirmed its presence with the crucifix and the Bible, Jake knew it had been exposed before it was ready. And for that, it would strike hard with a vengeance.

16

Jake had the rest of the afternoon at the house while Trevor was at work, and he could no longer focus on his clients and emails. The news from Arthur Briggs had made him uneasy and desperate for more information.

He searched for the website that Kelly had found before he'd left. The Spirit Seekers.

The familiar black page loaded, and pictures of Trevor and his two colleagues, Roger and Keith, appeared on his screen. At the bottom of the site was an email and a phone number. Jake opted to call.

He paced around the living room as the phone rang in his ear, on and on with no answer. He wondered if it was an office. Surely not. There was no way these guys could sit around all day long waiting for calls from potential clients. Or whoever it was they thought might contact them.

Jake hung up and frowned. Maybe an email would have to do.

Then his phone buzzed in his hands. A call returning from the one he'd just dialed.

"Hello?"

"Who is this?" The voice on the other line was low and suspicious.

"I found your number on your website. Spirit Seekers, right?"

"Yes," said the other man. "I haven't heard this phone ring in a long time."

"Oh. Well, my name is Jake Nolan, and my brother is Trevor Nolan. Your partner." There was silence for so long that Jake thought they'd gotten disconnected. "Are you there?"

"Yes, I'm here. It's just that Trevor's never mentioned before that he had a brother."

"Figures. We were a bit estranged until recently."

"Oh."

"I was calling to see if you could help me."

"The Spirit Seekers are kind of on hiatus right now."

"I'm not trying to be a client," Jake said. He wasn't sure what the Spirit Seekers did, exactly. "I want to talk to you guys about my brother. And about the house he's moved into."

Again, the other man was quiet for a long time, before saying, "Jake, is it okay if I call you back?"

"I guess so."

"Thanks. Give me a few minutes." He hung up without saying anything else.

Jake lowered the phone and shook his head. *Very strange.* But then again, what was he to expect? He was dealing with weirdos who most likely thought chasing ghosts was a game.

Just when he was thinking the man he'd spoken to had no intention of ever returning his call, his phone vibrated on the table. Jake answered it on the first ring.

"Can you meet today?"

The man's voice was serious and grave, and the request took Jake off guard. "Yeah, I guess so. Where?"

"There's a small restaurant called Captain's Arms. Next to the used car lot. Do you know the place?"

"I can find it." It didn't sound familiar. Must have been new.

"Meet us there in twenty minutes."

"Us?"

"Yes. Me and my partner, Keith."

"Oh." He must have been speaking with Roger this whole time. "Is everything okay?"

"I think it's best if we discuss all this in person," Roger said. "Twenty minutes. I'm leaving work now." Then he hung up.

Leaving work?

Jake wasn't sure what he'd stirred up, but apparently Roger felt it was important.

Maybe they had the advice he was looking for.

"Linda!" Jake called up the stairs. She'd gone into their bedroom. "I'm heading into town for a while."

She came out onto the landing and looked down. "Okay. Everything all right?"

"Yes, fine," he said, not sure if that was true.

"Will you be home for dinner?"

He told her he would, then left through the front door, using his phone to look up directions to Captain's Arms as he walked toward his rental car.

THE RESTAURANT TURNED out to occupy the building that had been a light fixture specialty store that Mom liked when Jake had been younger. He remembered having to go there with her on the weekend sometimes, bored out of his mind while she looked at lamps, usually never buying anything. At the time, though, Jake and Trevor had been happy to get out of the house and away from Dad. The used car lot next door was now empty, nothing more than a gravel wasteland.

The restaurant was dim and smelled of fried food and grease. Besides a single old man in the corner eating by himself, there were only two other customers.

They stood when Jake entered and introduced themselves.

Roger was shorter than Keith and wore an oversized, off-the-rack suit. Although his head was large, his eyes were small, with equally small glasses. His grey hair was neatly combed and in place and a well-maintained goatee framed his thin lips.

Keith was a foot taller and wore a short-sleeved button up plaid shirt and khaki cargo shorts. Stubble consumed his face and his skin was loose and wrinkled, with greasy hair. Whatever his job was, it was way less formal than Roger's. Perhaps he was unemployed.

They all sat down. Jake was across the table from the other two men, like it was a job interview.

But when Jake saw their faces, he knew this was far from a simple social call.

"Definitely Trev's brother," Keith said, glancing at

Roger. He pointed a long finger toward Jake. "You can see it in the eyes and nose."

"Ah yeah," Roger said. "I wonder why Trevor never mentioned you before."

"We kind of fell out as we grew older."

"So you were there?" Keith asked, eyebrows shooting up. "In that house when the haunting occurred?"

"I was there," Jake said. "I was the first one to see anything out of the ordinary. Trevor didn't believe me for the longest time." Roger and Keith exchanged a glance. "You mean Trevor never told you the story? I thought you guys were supposed to be paranormal investigators or whatever."

"Not really investigators," Roger said. "We are just interested in the paranormal."

"And Trev told us some of the story," Keith said. His voice was surprisingly high-pitched for his tall, lanky frame. "Although he never liked to talk about it much. It messed him up, from what I could tell."

"Maybe you can fill us in?" Roger asked. He clasped his hands in front of his round body on the table, and Jake wondered if this was how he spoke to people at work. He figured he was trying to put on a professional air, but there was a fear behind his eyes that Jake picked out immediately.

So Jake indulged them. Told them both everything he could from the best of his memory. The two men listened raptly.

"Yeah, that's way more than what Trevor ever told us," Keith said.

"Because Trevor didn't even know we were haunted until that summer was almost over," Jake said.

"And now he's gone back," Roger shook his head. "Crazy guy." He glanced at Keith. "Have you talked to Trev since then?"

"Nah. You?"

"So you three must not speak that much anymore," Jake said.

Roger shrugged. "The Spirit Seekers have mostly fallen apart these days. Life and real jobs get in the way, you know?"

"Yeah. And not to mention Trevor."

Jake perked up. "What about him?"

"He's been kind of…" Keith trailed off and looked to Roger for help.

"Not been himself," Roger said. Jake figured he also practiced that same beating around the bush at his office job.

"I've only been in town for a day and I've already seen his mood bounce all over the place," Jake said. "First, he's fine, then he's irritable, then he's very pissed off."

"Yeah," Keith said, leaning forward. "That's it."

"It all started about the time he told us he bought the old house," Roger said. He removed his glasses and wiped them on a piece of cloth from his coat pocket. "He couldn't wait to introduce us to his childhood home since it was so haunted." Roger returned the glasses to the bridge of his nose.

"Then what happened?" Jake asked.

"Went there, found nothing," Keith said. He leaned back again and crossed one long, dangling leg over the other. "Like, I mean, absolutely nothing. First time I ever felt dumb standing in the dark in the middle of the night trying to pick up an EVP."

"We tried to tell him nothing was there," Roger said, "but he wouldn't hear it. You should've heard how mad he got at that."

"He finally triggered some paranormal activity for the first time last night," Jake said.

Roger and Keith both stared at him.

"What happened?" Keith asked.

Jake told them about the crucifix and the Bible.

"Sounds like the ghost is mad at God," Keith said, a smirk on his face.

Jake found it refreshing that he didn't have to convince the two men that what he said was true. Speaking with believers was not something he was ever used to.

Keith looked at Roger. "Should we give him a call? If he's got some positive results, then it could be interesting."

Roger grimaced and shrugged.

"Do you guys know a man named Arthur Briggs?" Jake asked. He saw the name recognition dawn on them at the same time.

"Oh yeah," Keith said. "He's the real deal."

"What do you mean?"

"He's been dealing with the supernatural for a while. Was a priest in town for most of his life until he started flying around the country helping people with their ghost problems."

"Keith says he's the real deal because he refuses to associate with us," Roger said. "We've contacted him several times wanting to work with him, but he always tells us to give it up."

"Yeah. He takes it very seriously," Keith said. "Says there's no room for hobbyists like Roger and myself."

Jake agreed with Arthur Briggs. "I emailed him earlier, and he responded."

Roger sat up straighter. "He answered you? That easily?"

"He told me that what we have is a demon, not a ghost. That's why it doesn't like the religious objects. And we should get out of the house as soon as possible."

A silence fell over the table for a long while. Somewhere in the kitchen, someone dropped a glass that shattered.

"Never encountered a demon doing this," Keith said. "Don't know much about it. But if that's coming from Briggs, maybe you ought to —"

"There was one reason I never went back to that house," Roger said suddenly. Both Jake and Keith looked at him. The man slouched in his chair now, arms pulled tight against his body. Beads of sweat lined his forehead. "I never told Trevor, and I never told you either, Keith. It was easier to say I didn't think a spirit was in the house and that was my reason for not wanting to go back. But that isn't the truth. And this is why I felt it was important to meet with you in person, Jake." He swallowed heavily. "There is definitely something evil inside there."

Keith gave Roger a long look. "Why did you tell me you didn't think there was anything?"

"Because I was the only one who sensed something was wrong at the time," Roger explained. "That last night we were there. It was a Friday and we tried to get any paranormal reaction from whatever Trevor claimed lived in that house. Do you remember what time we left, Keith?"

"No."

"Three o'clock in the morning. Exactly."

"That's the time I always used to wake up when I was a kid," Jake said. "Every night."

"Demons love the number three," Roger said. "It mocks the Holy Trinity."

Keith's mouth turned into a thoughtful frown. "Really?"

The knocks always used to come in threes, Jake realized. Both during that summer and earlier at the house.

"Anyway," Roger said. "It was three o'clock in the morning and we decided to pack it in and leave. Trevor was being a nuisance because he was angry that we didn't have any evidence to show for our time. And as I was leaving, I remember getting this very distinct feeling..."

He trailed off, and the other two waited for him to pick up the story.

"What feeling?" Keith prodded.

"Hard to explain. A sense that I wasn't welcome there. Like I was intruding. Like I was hated."

"Yeah," Jake said. "That's the same feeling I get when I go inside the house."

The same thing he experienced when he was eight. Roger eyed him. "As if there's someone else there that you can't see. Watching you from around the corner, trying to make you leave with pure hatred alone."

"Exactly." It surprised Jake how accurately Roger could explain it.

Keith glanced back and forth between the two. "I never got that feeling when I was there."

"I remember how real it felt," Roger said, balling his fist and pressing it into his chest. "It was right here. A heavy pressure. I was sure that if I ever came back, then something horrible would happen, even though I had no way of knowing what."

"Why didn't you mention this before?" Keith asked.

"Because it was just something inside me," Roger said. "At the time, I explained it away. But if there really is a cruel spirit that haunts that house, even though I didn't see it, I experienced it."

"Imagine living there and having that feeling every day of your life," Jake said.

Roger leaned forward. "You've got to get your brother out of the house. Listen to Arthur Briggs. You can't stay there."

"Easier said than done," Jake said. "Trevor can be very stubborn."

"Oh, I know. But please. You're here for a reason, right? You came here because you understand how much danger he's in, didn't you?"

Jake nodded.

"Do whatever you must to get him out of there," Roger said. "If the supernatural activity is starting up after being silent for so long, then you might be running out of time."

17

That night, Trevor returned from work and Jake met him at the door before Linda could realize he was home. "I need to talk to you as soon as possible." He had already decided not to tell his brother that he'd met with Roger and Keith. That was likely to anger him.

"About what?"

"About what's going on in this house."

"Don't worry," Trevor said. "I have a plan." He nodded toward the box he carried.

"What's in there?"

Trevor held it out and Jake opened the flaps. It looked like he'd looted a Catholic church. Inside were many statues of crosses, all different shapes and sizes. Some had Jesus on them, others not. Among the crosses were small, pocket-size Bibles and candles.

"No. You can't do this."

"I have to."

"Trevor, I found the ladder turned upside down today. It was balancing on its own. How does that even happen?"

"Sounds like the kind of thing we got beaten for when we were kids."

"Exactly. And there's something else. Do you remember the guy who came to the house to cleanse it? Mom called him. His name was Arthur Briggs."

"Yes, of course."

"Well, he's still around. I emailed him about what happened last night. He told us to get the hell out of here as soon as possible. He said this is not a ghost, but an inhuman spirit. A demon."

Trevor's face remained empty, as if he was not even listening. Distracted.

"Trevor," Jake said. "A demon. It's not here just to be here. It plans on hurting you and your family."

"Whatever it is, it has to go," Trevor said.

"No, Trevor. *We* have to go. Have you ever encountered a demon in your paranormal investigating side thing?"

"No."

"Then you are not prepared to handle this. Do you remember? This thing wanted to hurt us and get us in trouble. It wanted Mom and Dad to fight and — "

And then his brother rounded on him. His eyes and nostrils flared and his face turned red with anger. "Shut the hell up and stop telling me what to do with my house and family." Jake backed away. Trevor dropped the box with a crash and advanced on his brother, puffing out his chest and clenching his fists. "I'll not have some little shit like you coming in here and getting in the way of what I know I have to do."

In that moment, Jake saw what Linda meant about Trevor's rapidly changing tempers. He'd never been afraid of his brother, but his fists were clenched, muscles taught, ready to defend himself if necessary.

"If you can't handle it, then get the hell out." Trevor picked the box back up and stormed up the stairs.

The tension ebbed from Jake's body as he watched him go. And couldn't help but notice that in that moment of outburst, Trevor had an uncanny resemblance to their father.

THE FOUR OF them had dinner an hour later. Linda had spent the afternoon making roast beef, and the whole time, Jake prayed that nothing crazy or supernatural would happen.

"And then we did math," Daniel said, telling about his day at school. "We're learning fractions. It's very hard."

"Your dad is great at math," Linda said. "Aren't you, Trevor?"

Trevor only grunted, not making eye contact. He still seethed after his confrontation with Jake earlier. Jake caught Linda frowning at her husband.

The conversation fell quiet after that. Daniel also glanced expectantly toward his father, perhaps hoping that he would offer to help him with his math problems, but nothing came. Trevor only chewed and stared at his plate.

Jake was struck by the similarity between how Trevor behaved now and how Dad had acted. It shocked him that his brother didn't recognize what was happening.

Then Daniel said, "What is Mama's cunt?"

Trevor looked up from his food for the first time, his eyes wide. Linda dropped her fork and it clattered to the ground. She gaped at her son. "What did you just say?"

Daniel recoiled in his chair. "Nothing."

"Daniel," Linda said, her voice rising. "Where did you learn that word?"

"I'm sorry," he blurted, fast becoming upset. "I didn't —"

"Did you hear it at school? Did one of the other boys say that to you?"

He clammed up.

Jake and Trevor locked eyes. Jake's heart sank as unpleasant and terrifying memories gurgled up inside of him. He could see by the look on his brother's face that he was experiencing the same.

"Trevor!" Linda whirled around. "Say something! Did you hear the filth that came out of your son's mouth?"

Daniel glanced back and forth between his mother and father, tears welling up.

As Jake and Trevor stared at each other, Jake noticed a change come over his brother. Color returned to his pale skin, his unfocused eyes cleared, as if coming out of a trance. He blinked slowly, realizing the implications of what Daniel had just said.

Whatever had oppressed him since he came home was momentarily gone.

"Linda," Trevor said calmly. "Wait."

"Wait? Why are you telling me to wait! You've sat there quiet all night and now you won't even address this either? Do something about your son!"

Trevor set his fork down and stood. His tall and wide

body imposed over them, making even Jake feel tiny. But his demeanor was completely calm. "Daniel. Please tell me where you heard that word."

Daniel only trembled in his chair.

"Answer your father," Linda chided.

Trevor held up a hand to her. "Daniel, you're not in trouble. I promise. But I do need to know where you learned that word."

A new glimmer of hope blossomed on Daniel's face, but he still did not respond.

"I think I know what's going on," Trevor said. "You didn't hear the word. You read it." Daniel nodded. "Where did you read it?" Daniel again did not want to answer.

Trevor went around the table and crouched down next to his son, took his hands in his own. Jake had never seen him act like such a father before. "Daniel." Now Trevor seemed like the one who was afraid. "Please. Show me."

Daniel must have realized his father would not let it drop. He slid off the chair and led Trevor upstairs. Linda and Jake followed behind.

He brought them to his bedroom — what had once been Jake and Trevor's. On the far wall, near the window that looked out to the old tree house, someone — or something — had written with a black crayon.

FUCK YOUR MOTHERS CUNT

IT WAS SCRAWLED IN JAGGED, barely legible handwriting. Underneath was a crude drawing of a woman with oversized breasts and her legs spread wide.

Linda gasped and pulled Daniel out of the room, covering his eyes.

Jake and Trevor stood together, staring. For them, this was a familiar message.

"Daniel!" Linda shouted. "What did you do?"

"Linda," Trevor warned again. "It wasn't him."

She glared at him. "Who was it? You?"

"Please calm down."

"Don't tell me to calm down! Do you see what your son drew on the wall?"

Trevor buried his face in his hands, pressing his fingers into his temples as if warding off a coming headache. "Daniel, you will sleep in the guest room tonight. Jake, you don't mind taking the couch, do you?" Jake shook his head. "Good. Daniel, why don't you take your pajamas into the hallway bathroom and get changed. It's time for bed."

"Can I bring my pillow with me?" Daniel asked.

"Of course."

Daniel retrieved his pajamas and his favorite pillow and disappeared into the bathroom.

"Do you mind telling me what's going on?" Linda asked, hands on her hips.

"It's the entity that lives here," Trevor said.

After Jake's previous discussion with Linda, he already knew how this would go over.

Linda rolled her eyes. "Trevor, I've never gotten in the way of you and your hobby, but come on. Enough is enough. You mean to tell me a *ghost* wrote that on Daniel's wall?"

"Yes. Do you think Daniel did it?"

That caused Linda to stumble on her words. "Well… I

would have thought not, but what other explanation is there?"

"I just gave it to you."

Linda huffed and glanced at Jake. Trevor turned to his brother and said, "Would you give us a few minutes?"

Jake nodded and made himself scarce. He removed his few belongings from the guest room as Daniel was getting under the covers.

"Don't worry about anything, buddy," Jake told him. "Your father has this under control." Even though that wasn't exactly true.

The boy was still frightened and confused. Even as Jake tried to reassure him, they could both hear Trevor and Linda's heated argument down the hall.

Jake turned out the lights, closed the door, and went downstairs. Behind him, Linda shouted at Trevor about scrubbing the writing off the wall, and Trevor insisting it wouldn't matter, that it would only return.

Linda couldn't grasp that, but it was true.

It's back. And the family is fighting. This is what it wants.

18

Jake tried his best to make himself comfortable on the couch. He was too tall, so he had to keep his knees bent.

He fell asleep on his back, although it was a light and uncomfortable sleep, prone to strange dreams where his new apartment was vandalized and destroyed.

Jake woke up suddenly and all at once. His eyes opened as if a switch had been flipped inside him. He sat up and looked around the room, at first not remembering where he was.

Oh, right. Trevor's living room. It was so dark he could barely see in front of his face.

He checked the time on his phone and the bright light burned his eyes as they adjusted. It was exactly three o'clock in the morning.

Jake gasped. That was a time he knew well from the past — when Trevor would get out of bed and wander around.

Jake lay back on the couch, trying to force himself to

go back to sleep, to convince himself that waking up at three o'clock was just a coincidence.

But it isn't. That thing wants me awake right now. Every night he awoke at that time when he was a child, there was always a reason.

Something was about to happen.

Jake felt a cool breeze blow across his warm face as if a window had been opened. He looked around the room — all the windows were closed. But then he noticed the front door of the house hung wide open.

Jake stepped out onto the porch, just to check, but there was nothing to see. So he went back inside and shut the door behind him.

Then he remembered.

A strong gut feeling propelled him forward. He opened the door again and rushed down the front porch steps, then around to the backyard. And in the darkness he saw it.

Daniel was climbing the tree, up toward the old tree house.

"No!" Jake called out. He ran over to the trunk and shouted up at the boy. "Daniel! Come down!"

But Daniel made no indication that he had heard him.

Jake gripped the wooden planks that formed the ladder and went up after him. He was about a hundred pounds more than the last time he'd attempted to climb, and the old wood felt weak and flaky underneath his bare feet.

Daniel climbed deftly, controlled by something else. He made it to the top branch and walked with perfect balance toward the dark, old tree house.

Halfway up the tree, Jake was stopped. The force bore

down on him, preventing him from moving forward, keeping him at bay.

The same thing repeating itself seventeen years later.

"Give him back!" he shouted at whatever was there, blocking his way up. "Take me, not him!"

Jake was stronger now than he was then. He forced himself upward, plowing through the invisible force. It was like trying to move on another planet that had gravity three times stronger than Earth.

When he reached the branch, the force let go. Jake crawled along in the dark, striving to not lose his balance. He knew at any moment, the thing could push him out of the tree.

Daniel stood in the center of the tree house now — the same position Trevor had been in when Dad had caught them and beaten them.

Jake made it to the tree house and rushed inside, scraping his scalp against the short doorframe. He scooped up Daniel in his arms. The boy was dead weight and heavier than he'd expected. His eyes were open, but lost in the trance.

Jake brought Daniel to the ladder and tossed him over his shoulder. He carefully climbed down, keeping a good grip with one hand while balancing Daniel with the other.

"Don't worry buddy," he said to the boy. "We'll get you down. You'll be safe."

Jake was halfway down the ladder when the push came. He fell backwards into thin air, and as he did, he shifted Daniel to the top of this chest. He hit the ground, absorbing all impact through his back. His head collided with the ground, sending a shock of pain through his brain.

Daniel jolted awake. Jake's sternum felt close to being crushed by the weight of the boy landing hard on top of him.

Daniel looked around, confused.

Jake groaned in pain.

"What's going on?" Daniel asked. He rubbed his head, the part that had collided with Jake's chest.

"Don't worry," Jake said. "I've got you." His words were weak as the air had been knocked out of his lungs. His vision was blurred.

When his sight cleared, Jake saw something hovering near the tree trunk where he'd been pushed. A black shadow, darker than the surrounding night. Although it had no definite shape, it still resembled the silhouette of a person.

Jake's mouth went dry. He wanted to scream, but couldn't. He was unable move, frozen in place by the same invisible force that had tried to keep him from climbing the tree.

Held down and at the mercy of the demon above him.

19

Help.

Still no words escaped from his frozen throat, his locked mouth. Then there were other voices and footsteps.

"What's going on out here?" Linda.

"Jake! Daniel! What are you doing?" Trevor.

The shadow vanished and Jake found he could move again.

He felt Daniel lifted off his body, giving him welcome relief from his weight. Strong arms grabbed him under his armpits, hauling him up to his feet, but he couldn't support himself. He was dragged into the house.

By the time Jake fully realized what was happening, he was on the couch with Trevor handing him a towel filled with ice.

He pressed it to the back of his head. It stung.

Linda sat on the chair on the other side of the living room, Daniel on her lap. She inspected him for injuries, but there were none. Jake had taken the full impact of the fall.

"Jake," Trevor said, his face close to his. "What happened?"

Jake's clarity slowly returned. Then he said, "You already know."

Trevor did not respond.

"I don't understand," Linda said, hysterical. "Daniel, what were you doing up in that tree house? And in the middle of the night? Do you realize how dangerous that was? You could have really hurt yourself!"

"Linda," Trevor said. "It wasn't him."

And Linda gave him a look. Once again, Daniel was not to blame.

"Don't start this again," she demanded.

"Why was I outside?" Daniel asked.

"You don't remember?" Daniel shook his head. "You must have been sleepwalking."

"He wasn't sleepwalking," Jake said, forcing himself to sit up on the couch. His entire body ached and his brain throbbed. "Trevor used to do the same thing when we were younger."

"Why Daniel?" Trevor asked. "I don't understand. I'm the one it wanted all those years ago."

"It isn't about you," Jake said, dropping the ice from the back of his head. "It's about children." Trevor and Linda glanced at each other. Linda, for the first time, looked afraid.

"Children," Trevor repeated.

"Everything that happened to you and me is happening to Daniel," Jake said. "It isn't interested in us."

"What wants me?" Daniel asked, his voice shaken and weak.

"Nothing, dear," Linda whispered in his ear. "Nothing will hurt you."

"Trevor, you *have* to get out of this house. I know what you thought would happen, but this thing doesn't play by your rules. It avoids you and only attacks Daniel."

"But — "

"No! Quit resisting this. Give it up and leave. Do it for your family."

"Stop!" Trevor bellowed. "You keep telling me to run away, but I won't. I've been tortured by this thing ever since we were kids. I need to *defeat* it. I can't be a coward like you!"

Jake's anger spiked. He shot to his feet and threw the towel angrily to the floor. Ice cubes scattered all across the hardwood. "It isn't about being a coward! It's about knowing when you've *lost*."

Then Trevor's hands were on him. Jake grappled back and the two brothers collapsed to the ground, wrestling. Jake saw Trevor's face twisted and red with anger, the oppressive fury returning.

"Stop it!" Linda shrieked at the top of her lungs.

Jake and Trevor released each other and separated. Jake sprawled on his back, breathless from the short tussle with his brother. Tears came to his eyes. *It's winning. This is what it wants.* He imagined the shadow standing nearby, invisible, laughing with glee at how it could tear apart a family.

"I don't understand what's going on anymore," Linda said, "but all I know is that if something is coming after Daniel, then I want to leave this house. Right now."

Jake and Trevor stared up at her from the floor. She stood with hands on hips while Daniel curled into a ball on the chair, afraid.

"But — "

"*Trevor*!"

The living room fell silent. All three of them watched Trevor where he sat. He took in the opposition, and finally nodded his head, sighing. "Fine."

Thirty minutes later, Linda had packed a bag for Daniel and herself while Trevor did his own. For Jake, it was only a matter of putting his few belongings into his carry-on.

"Where will you go?" Jake asked as Trevor slung the bags into the trunk of the family car.

"There's a cheap motel in town. You'll remember it."

Jake followed in his rental, and when they arrived, Jake did indeed recognize it from his youth. It was ratty back then, and now it was even more of a dive.

"You can't be serious," Linda said as she got out of the car, surveying the place.

"It's here or the house," Trevor said. Linda bit her lip.

Inside, Trevor booked a room for the family. Linda and Daniel waited on the opposite side of the lobby.

"And one for me as well," Jake said, stepping up to the counter.

"What will you do?" Trevor asked him.

Jake sighed. "I have to go home."

"Probably for the best."

"But you can't go back in that house."

Trevor glared at him, and Jake realized his brother had not planned on staying in that motel for long. "What am I supposed to do? That house cost me everything."

"I get that, but you have to figure it out. Money is nothing when it comes to that thing trying to attack Daniel."

Trevor looked away. The motel clerk shot them an odd glance as he typed their information into his computer.

"Just let it be," Jake said. "You tried."

Trevor's temples bulged as he ground his teeth.

Jake didn't know what to do or how to convince him. One thing was for sure — he couldn't stay in Rose Grove forever and babysit Trevor.

"I can't just let it be," Trevor said.

"Why?" Jake said with a burst of anger. "Why can't you just leave it again? I did."

"Because it won't let me!" Trevor shot back. His raised voice attracted confused stares from his wife and son.

He gripped Jake's arm and pulled him to the corner of the lobby, as far out of earshot as they could get from Linda and Daniel and the desk clerk.

"You think I haven't tried moving on?" Trevor forced his voice low. "That thing follows me around wherever I go."

Jake clenched his jaw closed. His brother turned away from him, rubbing a hand over his face, as if trying to make himself focus. "What do you mean?"

"I mean the paranormal activity happened to me even at our old house," Trevor said.

"But…"

"Yes. It can reach me even when I'm not living in the actual house. It's me and my family. Not the house. So what you said earlier about it only wanting children was wrong. It's going after Daniel now just to get to me. And it's working."

Jake remembered the airplane and the drive to town. Trevor was right. The thing could reach you wherever you were, if it wanted you.

"Linda's jewelry would disappear," Trevor went on. "Little messages appeared that I had to scrub out before Linda or Daniel saw them. The three knocks on the door in the middle of the night, but no one would be there. I eventually quit getting out of bed to check, but then they started to come from the roof over my bed."

"I don't get it," Jake said. He had not experienced any of those things since moving away from Rose Grove. That is, until he'd made the conscious decision to return to the town to help his brother. That was when the cockroach had fallen into Kelly's lap.

"It was only targeting me and not Linda or Daniel, thank God," Trevor said. "And it only began after I started going to church. The more frequently I went, the stronger the activity became."

That made sense to Jake, considering the way the demon reacted when religious objects were present. "So that's why you moved back," he said.

"I knew I couldn't just ignore it," Trevor said. "So I had to come back. Because if I let it go on too long, then eventually it would show itself to Linda and Daniel. And I couldn't have that."

"But now that's starting to happen anyway."

Trevor sighed. "At least being in that house gave me a chance to beat it."

After they got their keys and found their rooms, Linda pulled Jake aside while Trevor was in the bathroom. She folded her arms across her chest and her eyes were red and puffy from crying. "What will you do?"

"I'll leave in the morning. I have to get back to work."

She wiped a tear that escaped. "What's going on with my husband?"

"I know you don't believe," he said gently, "but it's all real. It might take time to accept that, but I wouldn't lie to you. You've seen the signs yourself." Linda licked her lips and looked away. "Be patient with him, but whatever you do, please don't return to the house. Definitely don't let Daniel go back in."

Linda nodded and took a deep breath. "I have no idea what we'll do next."

"You'll pull together," Jake said. "You got out in time." Unlike his own family. Dad had insisted they stay long after they should have fled. And look what happened to them.

"It was nice to finally meet you," Linda said. "I wish it could have been under better circumstances."

They hugged and retired to their respective rooms.

Inside, Jake threw open the covers of his bed and jumped when he saw the huge cockroach on the white bed sheet.

Sign of the demon or a dirty hotel room?

The cockroach scurried and forced itself under the pillow. Jake lifted it up, and it had disappeared.

20

1995

Summer was ending and Jake could not wait to go return to school. It was the first time he had ever felt that way. But going back would get him out of the house and away from Dad.

Trevor's sleepwalking continued. Jake was diligent and locked the bedroom door every night. At least three times a week, he would awaken to the sound of Trevor, asleep and in a trance, trying to open the door.

Jake would take his brother by the hand, and guide him back to bed. At first, Trevor would resist, but then the spirit would let him go.

Trevor never remembered the next day.

One morning in early August, Jake and Trevor sat at the breakfast table eating cereal. Mom was at home and Dad was at work. Jake hated to admit it, but it was his favorite time of day because Dad wasn't around. When evening approached, he grew nervous, never knowing what his father's mood would be.

Mom busied herself in the kitchen, washing dishes and wiping the countertop.

Jake concerned himself with his cereal, scooping up the last remaining bits that floated in the milk one at a time.

Trevor nudged him. He looked nervous.

"What?"

Trevor shot a finger to his lips and glanced to make sure Mom wasn't looking. He nodded his head toward the refrigerator.

Jake followed his signal, searching for what he saw. At first, nothing was out of place. The refrigerator surface was covered with pictures, good test grades from school, and post cards from their grandparents who lived in Texas.

And at the bottom, a bunch of colorful, magnetic letters and numbers. When they were younger, they would sit with Mom and practice spelling simple words on the refrigerator door. Now they caught Jake's eye. All the letters were pushed to form a circle, almost perfectly round. In the middle was a single phrase.

FUCK YOU

Jake looked at Trevor. His brother questioned him with a silent look, asking if Jake did it. Jake shook his head. Of course he didn't do it. The only time he'd ever heard that word was when Dad was really mad, and didn't even know what it meant — only that he was never supposed to say it.

And if Mom noticed, they'd get in huge trouble. If Dad did, they would be in a lot of pain.

Jake and Trevor sat rigidly in their chairs, holding their breath as Mom went to the fridge and put the milk back inside. She walked away, not noticing the vulgarity right beneath her line of sight.

Then, she left the kitchen.

Jake shot up from the chair and hurried over to the refrigerator, peeked into the living room to make sure Mom was gone, and then rearranged the letters, smearing them around.

"Who did that?" Trevor whispered.

"I don't know. Definitely not me."

"Not me either."

Jake believed him, but at the same time didn't. Maybe Trevor did it on one of his sleepwalking episodes. But he wasn't able to get out of the room. Perhaps he did it on the first night when he climbed to the tree house. How long had the letters been like that?

Two days later, as Jake and Trevor went into the kitchen for dinner, Mom and Dad already sat at the table. Jake passed by the fridge and saw the letters had been moved again.

YOURE A FUCKING COCKSUCKER

Jake looked around quickly, then shuffled the message.

Trevor must have been doing it but not remembering. But when?

After dinner, Jake told Trevor. "You have to stop doing that."

"It's not me!" Trevor shot back at him. "Why would I do that? Dad would get really mad. Maybe it's you!"

"No way!"

"If I get in trouble for you writing bad words on the

refrigerator, I'm going to break your arm. I mean it. This isn't funny. You know how Dad is now."

"It isn't me!"

Trevor got furious at that, not believing him. He even shoved him backward. Jake didn't fall, but he still felt very hurt. Trevor had never done that to him before.

The next night, at dinner, Jake checked the refrigerator again. It was becoming a habit to make sure Trevor wasn't leaving behind any messages that would get them in trouble.

They letters were rearranged within a perfect circle again.

HI

That was all it said.

Well, that isn't too bad, Jake thought. A lot better than what they were dealing with before.

So Jake left it. He joined his family at the table.

Halfway through the dinner, Dad told Jake to get him another beer.

Mom gave Dad a look, one that only happened between adults. He looked to his mother for permission even though he already knew what she would say. She nodded tentatively.

When he got to the fridge, the letters and been moved.

HE SHOULDNT DRINK SO MUCH

Jake gasped. A very cold feeling enveloped him.

He glanced back to his family in the dining room. The three of them ate silently, no one having gotten up from the table.

They moved on their own.

How was that even possible? And how did they know he was going to get a beer?

Jake scrambled the magnets again, the sounds of them scraping on the refrigerator door causing Dad's head to perk up. "What are you doing?" He shouted. "Bring me the beer!"

Jake grabbed one from the shelf inside the fridge.

After dinner, Jake made sure he was the first one to grab the plates and take them to the sink.

"Oh, thank you," Mom said, surprised by Jake's quick thoughtfulness. Dad gave him a suspicious look, and so did Trevor.

He went into the kitchen with the dirty dishes. The letters were back in place.

PLEASE TALK TO ME

The hair rose on the back of Jake's neck.

Jake put the plates in the dishwasher and returned to the fridge. He searched the jumble of letters and picked the ones he needed.

NO

He put it under the first message.

Mom started cleaning the dishes and Dad retired to the living room to watch television as he usually did.

Jake went upstairs to his bedroom. He wanted to tell Trevor about the messages appearing on the refrigerator throughout dinner, but Trevor would not believe him. Would likely only blame him again.

He felt truly alone in that house.

There was a loud crash and commotion downstairs. Jake heard Dad scream, "Oh, fuck!"

Something had fallen over in the kitchen. Mom had probably dropped something. Now Dad would get mad and yell at her. But then it came.

"Jake! Trevor!"

The two boys' heads shot up. Jake's gut clenched. With no choice, they trudged downstairs.

The loud crash had come from the refrigerator. The door was open and all the beers — at least ten cans — were on the ground, opened and sprayed all over the floor. Mom and Dad stood over it.

"Dad," Trevor began. "We were upstairs."

"Shut up," he said. He closed the refrigerator door. "What the hell is this?"

The messages Jake had left behind were replaced.

FUCK YOUR MOTHERS CUNT

Jake froze. He didn't know what that meant.

Mom gasped and covered her mouth. Jake figured it was something terrible. And he predicted what was coming next. Dad wasn't even mad about the beer.

"Dad, we didn't do it," Jake pleaded. "I swear."

"We were upstairs the whole time." Trevor added.

"Where did you learn to talk like this?" Dad bellowed.

"It wasn't us!"

"So you're saying your mother comes in here and writes these things on the door?"

"No!"

"Then what are you saying?"

"I don't know!" Jake was crying now. He couldn't help it. Even Trevor looked to be on the verge of tears.

In the end, Dad took Trevor over his knee and beat his behind so badly he couldn't even scream out in pain. He made Jake watch so he knew what was coming next.

And it came. Jake was vaguely aware of Mom calling out for Dad to stop, shouting that it was enough. Jake could've sworn he got beaten more than Trevor.

They were sent upstairs together and ordered not to

come out of the room. It was a punishment even worse than the spanking because Trevor rounded on him next.

"I told you to quit writing with the magnets!"

"It wasn't me," Jake said.

But Trevor didn't want to talk to him anymore. He crawled in bed and pulled the covers over his head.

"Please believe me," Jake whimpered, but there was no response.

In the morning, at breakfast, Jake made sure to get into the kitchen before anyone else. The letters were rearranged.

HA HA HA HA HU HU HU

Jake scraped all the magnets off the fridge and dumped them into one of the plastic grocery bags Mom kept beneath the sink. He went outside and around the back of the house, beyond the big tree to where the woods met the edge of their property.

He got down on his knees and dug a hole. The dirt ground into his fingernails, soft against his palm. At one point he even unearthed a worm.

When the hole was deep enough, Jake upended the bag of letters into a pile and covered them. Giving them their own shallow grave.

He brushed his hands off and returned to breakfast.

Mom noticed that the magnets were gone. She stared at the refrigerator for a few seconds and Jake waited for her to ask where they went, but she didn't.

Trevor noticed too, but said nothing.

21

1995

Three days later, Jake was watching television. Trevor walked into the room and stared at him for a few seconds.

"What?" Jake finally asked.

"I thought Mom and Dad took the magnets away."

It was the first time Trevor had mentioned their disappearance. "No. I did."

"Oh. Then why did you put them back?"

An empty, uneasy feeling sprouted in the pit of Jake's stomach. "What are you talking about? I didn't put them back." Then Jake realized that when it came to the ghost in their house, anything was possible.

Trevor said nothing. So Jake slid off the couch and followed his brother into the kitchen.

DONT DO THAT AGAIN YOU SHIT

The letters were covered in brown dirt.

Jake scrambled out the message. A sudden fit of frustration took him and he grabbed two handfuls of the magnets, ripped them from the refrigerator door, and slammed them onto the tiled floor as hard as he could.

Trevor didn't react to his outburst at all. "What's going on?"

Jake stared at his brother for a few moments. "You wouldn't believe me if I told you."

"Why did you put them back?" Trevor asked again.

"I already told you that I didn't!"

"Jake…" His face fell. "Come on."

"It's not me. It's the ghost."

Trevor's brow furrowed. "The ghost?"

"Yes. We have a ghost that lives in this house. And it's trying to get us into trouble."

Trevor sighed. "Whatever. I don't know why you keep writing this stuff on the refrigerator, but you have to stop. We're going to —"

But then the magnets started moving on their own. The ones that Jake had thrown to the floor lifted and zipped into place on the fridge, forming a new message within two seconds.

IM DOING IT TREVOR NOT JAKE HA HA HU HU

Trevor took a step back "Oh my god. Did you see that?"

Jake was equally as startled. Even though he knew the letters were moving by themselves, it was the first time he'd actually seen them in motion.

"How did they do that?" Trevor's eyes were wide.

The letters moved again.

NOT MOVING ON THEIR OWN HA HA HU HU

Trevor jumped back a few more paces. "Jake!" He pointed at the refrigerator, his hand trembling.

Jake wanted to say, "I told you so," but he was too afraid.

The letters whipped around again, rearranging themselves into a new message.

FUCK PISS SHIT COCK

Trevor ran to the fridge and scrambled them out. Dad passed by, walking into the living room. He didn't spot them there. He sat down heavily on the couch and turned on the television.

When Jake and Trevor turned back to the magnets, they had already moved again.

HE HATES YOU AND YOUR MOTHER

"A ghost…" Trevor whispered, staring at his brother, eyes pleading to be told it wasn't the truth. "How long have you known?"

"We have to get rid of them again," Jake said. But burying them didn't work. "I have an idea. Take them off the refrigerator and put them in a bag. Meet me in the backyard."

Trevor nodded, too stunned to protest.

Jake ran upstairs to the bedroom. Inside the closet, behind a pile of old shoes and toys was a hidden shoebox. This was his little safety box, filled with cash and coins, his personal savings account, one that not even Trevor knew about. He also had a few things in there Dad would consider contraband. At the bottom was a pack of matches and he shoved them in his pocket.

Trevor waited for him in the backyard, holding the plastic bag.

"I buried them out here," Jake said, leading Trevor to the spot. Sure enough, there was a hole in the ground that looked like it had been dug up by an animal. There were even claw marks. A shiver ran up Jake's spine, wondering what kind of horrible hands the ghost had. "We need leaves and sticks."

Trevor set the bag down and the two boys foraged through the woods behind the house and came up with the materials.

They arranged the leaves and twigs in the hole and Jake used the matches to start a small flame. Once it caught and was going well, Trevor fed larger sticks onto the top to keep the fire going.

Once it was burning, they opened the bag and tossed the magnets in the fire. The plastic melted and the colored paint seeped off. Black smoke rose into the air and the terrible smell forced Jake and Trevor to cover their noses with their shirts. Jake kept peeking over his shoulder, making sure no one was coming. If Dad saw them, they would be in big trouble.

After the last of the letters burned, Trevor returned to the house and brought back a cup of water. He used it to put out the flames, extinguishing it into a squelch of black smoke.

They scattered the ashes with their feet, hiding the evidence that there had ever been a fire.

"There," Jake said. "That should take care of that."

When he looked over to Trevor, his brother looked back at him as if he were ready to cry. Upset, confused, and frightened all at the same time. "A ghost?"

"Weird stuff has been happening all summer," Jake said weakly.

"Like what?"

"Like you sleepwalking in the middle of the night. Trying to climb up to the tree house."

Trevor rolled his eyes. "You're blaming the ghost?"

"What else could it be?"

"Maybe me just sleepwalking?"

"No," Jake said. "It's making you do things you normally wouldn't do. And it's making you act weird. Like you never want to go outside and play anymore."

"Because of my arm, genius."

"A broken arm doesn't mean you can't go outside and play."

Trevor huffed and turned away from him. Jake could see that Trevor didn't want to believe, but he was having a hard time coming to terms with what he had just seen.

"How do you explain the magnets moving on their own?" Jake said.

"I don't know," Trevor said, although Jake could see he was trying his best to resist the idea. "I don't believe in any of that stuff. It's stupid."

"And..."

"And what?"

Jake had just been about to tell him that he believed the ghost had pushed him out of the tree, but caught himself. He could tell just how upset Trevor was.

"I don't want to think about this anymore," Trevor said. He whirled around and stomped through the backyard back to the house.

Jake let him go.

What frightened Jake the most about what had just happened was the ghost had, for the first time, revealed itself to Trevor. Surely that was part of some strategy it had. It no longer wanted to torment Jake alone, and was ready to expand its plan. It wanted to attack Trevor directly as well.

And Jake knew that meant things would only get worse.

After that day, the letters did not return to the refrigerator as they had when Jake had buried them. Neither Mom nor Dad asked what had happened to them.

22

2018

These were the first nights Kelly had spent alone in a long time.

Before, she had roommates. Even though she'd had her own room, there was at least one person around should something go wrong. Then, she'd moved in with Greg. After they broke up, it was back with the roommates. Jake came along, and once they got serious, more often than not, she would sleep at his house or him at hers.

She'd gotten used to not being alone at night, and she found she was still uncomfortable with it.

She was in bed with the lamp on. It was not something she usually did, but given the circumstances of Jake being absent, she made an exception.

Haunted.

She'd had plenty of quiet time to think about Jake and what he was doing by rushing home to Rose Grove.

Deal with the haunting? Protect his brother from a ghost?

She'd never really believed in stuff like that. If Jake did, that was fine, given he had experiences when he was younger that made him feel ghosts were real. But if it was something that would cause stress in their relationship, then she knew they needed to deal with it now instead of later.

Especially if this haunting causes him to clam up about his past.

She thought of ghosts and zombies and monsters, all images that kept her up throughout the night. In the morning, she went to work and relied on coffee to get her through the day.

When she came home, she planned to take a nap, but by the time she laid on the couch, she found she was wide awake again.

She picked up her cell phone and tried to call Jake, but he did not answer. It was the second attempt, and he had not returned that call either.

Kelly grabbed her laptop and navigated back to the website that Trevor Nolan ran. She'd bookmarked it after Jake had gone. The blog, however, was not updated.

The phone rang, the shrill chirping sounds startling her. She checked the screen, hoping for Jake, but it was her mother.

"Hey Mom."

"Hey there. How are you?"

"Good. The apartment's done and we're all moved in."

"Is everything going… okay?"

Kelly had filled her mom in on her reservations about moving in with another guy. "Yeah. So far so good."

"Really?"

There must have been something in her tone that gave her away. Her mother was great at picking up on those things. "Well…"

"What's going on? Tell me."

"I figured out what the deal is with Jake's family."

"He told you?"

"No. I just kind of stumbled on it."

"What is it?"

When Kelly told her, she felt extremely silly saying it.

"The line must have cut out," her mother said. "Did you say haunted?"

"Yes." Her mother was silent for a long time. "He believes his childhood home was haunted."

"Well… at least it wasn't something serious."

"That's what I thought too, but whatever happened messed him up," Kelly said. "So if it's serious to him then it needs to be serious to me."

"How did this all come up?" she asked.

Kelly told her the story about finding the photograph and newspaper article, and Jake's subsequent rushing off to Rose Grove.

"You're telling the truth? He ran off to Georgia to deal with a haunted house?"

"When you put it like that…"

"There's no other way to say it," her mother said, growing stern. "This is a little weird, Kelly. Maybe your gut was right when it told you to hold off moving in with him so quickly."

"It's not like that, Mom," Kelly said, although it wasn't entirely true. "I want to help him if I can."

"Sounds like he needs a therapist."

"Give him more time," Kelly said. "We can work this out."

Her mother sighed. "If you say so. You know how I feel about the whole situation." She paused. "Have you heard from Greg?"

"Mom!"

"Just asking."

"No, I have not."

Her mother was Greg's biggest fan, and no one decried the end of their relationship more than her. She'd refused to accept that Greg had anything negative about him, no matter how much Kelly tried to convince her.

"Well maybe…"

"Get over it, Mom. I'm with Jake now, and he's a much better match for me." *Even though there's this whole haunting thing.* "Look, I have to run. I'll talk to you later."

Kelly knew her mother wasn't ready to hang up yet, but she let her go anyway. Discussing the situation with her made her feel dumb and wasn't helpful in the least. Which made her wonder what, if anything, would be helpful to her in that moment.

Jake answering the phone would be a start.

She reached for her laptop again, which was half folded closed. When she opened it, a massive, brown cockroach rested on the keys.

Kelly shrieked and pushed the computer away from her. It clattered on the floor, sending the bug scurrying.

She remembered what happened last time, and forced herself to calm down and watch the thing crawl across the carpet. It disappeared around the corner and into the kitchen.

Kelly shot off the couch and chased after it, but when

she got there, it had vanished — just as she predicted it would. Like last time.

And once again, Kelly reconsidered where she drew the line between reality and the supernatural.

Why is this happening? Jake isn't here...

She would have to tell him about it when he returned her call.

Her phone rang, startling her again. She crossed the room and picked it up from the coffee table, once again expecting Jake, but instead got a bigger surprise.

Greg.

She held the phone in her palm, watching it ring, unable to remember the last time she'd seen Greg's name appear on her screen. Her heart thudded in her throat, and already she was disappointed in herself for not immediately declining the call.

What is this? It was too much to be a mere coincidence.

And before she knew what was happening, she answered the phone.

23

Jake trudged through the airport, tired and annoyed from the flight. Everything went wrong — they'd booked him in the incorrect seat, the armrest didn't fold down, and the headphones had not worked in one ear. Normally, all of those things would have been minor annoyances only, but that day, it all really irritated him.

Kelly met him near the exit. When she saw him, she went to embrace him, but the smile soon melted from her face. "Jake, are you okay?"

"It's been a long few days."

"You look… different."

"How?" Jake clenched his teeth. The last thing he wanted was to be scrutinized.

"I don't know… just…"

"Well, you try spending the night in a haunted house," he snapped. "Let me know how it feels." He brushed past her and headed toward the parking garage.

Kelly said nothing else on the ride home.

When they arrived, Jake realized he was being mean. "I'm sorry," he told Kelly. "I think I just need to sleep."

"We can talk about it if you want." She looked at him, concerned.

"No. I need to lie down."

"Sure."

Jake trudged to the bedroom and collapsed on top of the covers. His eyelids were heavy — he'd not gotten much sleep the past few days. But now that he was down and in his own bed, where he thought he'd be most comfortable, he couldn't drift off. Instead his brain worked overtime. He wondered what Trevor would do, and if he would try to go back to the house.

Greg was here.

Jake shot up. The thought ran through his mind like a passing race car, there one moment and gone the next. He didn't know where it came from either — as if someone had opened his brain and dumped it there.

I guess he could have been while I was there, he thought. A perfect time for Kelly to catch up with her ex-boyfriend, who he sometimes felt she still missed. He laid back down and tried to forget it. *No. It's the demon doing this to me.*

It made Trevor behave much the same way. Now it was trying to oppress him too even though he was far away. Like some sort of lasting, residual effect from having been in its presence.

I'll get through it. Won't let these feelings get me down.

But no matter how hard he tried, he couldn't fall back asleep. Every time he closed his eyes, he saw the black shadow, staring at him, hating him, waiting for the perfect opportunity to attack him again.

JAKE SAT in his cubicle at work. The sounds of the office were a dull song in the background — the ringing phones, the printer running off a hundred copies, and the muffled conversations at the surrounding desks.

His face was in his hands, unable to concentrate on any tasks. In fact, since he had returned to work two weeks ago, he'd accomplished almost nothing. And his boss definitely noticed.

The phone rang, the shrill ringtone snapping him out of his trance, startling him. It had been changed, which meant someone used his desk while he was away. A sudden, inexplicable rage boiled inside of him. *Frank. He's always after my desk. Says his is underneath the air conditioning vent.* He'd have to have a stern word with Frank later.

Jake snatched the phone from the cradle but managed to get his anger under control before speaking. "Jake Nolan."

"Jake," said Mr. Allen, his boss.

"Mr. Allen. Hi. How are you?"

"Good. Are you free right now?"

"Yes."

"Can you come to my office?"

Jake's stomach sank. *Did I forget to do something while I was away?* "Sure."

"Great. See you in a minute."

As he walked through the maze of other cubicles, his mind raced. Yeah, he'd fallen behind with work while he was gone and hadn't caught up since he'd been back.

Hopefully it would just be a slap on the wrist. The secretary gestured for him to go straight in.

"Please, sit down," Mr. Allen said.

Jake did, and Mr. Allen sat down in the seat across the desk. Jake could already tell by the look on his face that there wasn't good news.

"Jake," Mr. Allen began, folding his hands in front of him, not meeting him in the eye. "Is everything okay at home?"

"Yes, sir."

"I know you took some emergency time off. You came back sooner than expected. Are you sure everything is fine?"

"Yes, sir," Jake said, although he could tell Mr. Allen did not believe him. Jake was well aware he looked tired, haggard, and his clothes were wrinkled, untucked and disheveled. He hadn't shaved, either. The days in Rose Grove took its toll on him more than he cared to admit.

"Well," Mr. Allen went on, "I can't force you to divulge your personal life, and I do not want you to if you aren't comfortable. That being said, there has been a notable decrease in your performance the last two weeks."

Jake only stared ahead. It was true after all.

"Unfortunately, this was a critical time for us. You know we have many big clients right now and all of those deadlines are coming up. While you were gone, Craig took on a lot of your work and got it done. I'm afraid we had to put him in charge of the projects associated with these clients."

Jake sat there silent. At first he didn't hear it, but then it registered. "You gave my promotion to Craig?"

Jake even liked Craig. He was a good guy and a hard

worker, but he had been at the company for less time than him.

"It's not that you're a poor employee," Mr. Allen said. "It was the unfortunate timing of your circumstances. We had to… move on with someone else. I hope you understand. As soon as a new position opens up, it's yours. I'm sorry to have to give you this news."

Jake said nothing. He slowly blinked once as the weight of the world come down on him, pressing him into that comfortable leather chair opposite his boss's desk. It would be at least another year before a promotion became available again.

The reason he and Kelly had settled on that apartment was because they were counting on Jake's salary to increase. It was his, and it had slipped away at the last second.

All because of that fucking demon. No wonder Kelly still loves Greg.

Jake caught himself and forced the thought down.

Jake thanked Mr. Allen for his time and returned to his desk and tried to come up with a way to tell Kelly the news.

24

The phone rang and rang, but Jake did not answer so Kelly hung up.

She frowned. He had not been the same since he had returned from Rose Grove two and a half weeks ago. He spent the evenings moping around, not talking or looking her in the eye, going to bed early, then waking up late for work.

She had tried everything to get through to him but nothing was working.

What happened while he was there? It reminded her of some sort of PTSD.

Kelly set her phone down and turned to her computer. She was at work and had free time while her third graders were at lunch, so she found Trevor Nolan's paranormal website and went back to his blog. It had been updated recently.

MY BROTHER ARRIVED YESTERDAY. He found this site, along with a newspaper article about how Linda and I had bought our childhood home, which had been uninhabited since my family moved out when I was twelve years old.

As most of you know from my previous posts, this house is haunted. The ghost inside was the reason for my family's dysfunction, and why my parents split up. I also blame the ghost for my father's early death from alcoholism and my mother's suicide. The things that occurred to us while we lived in here were traumatic and horrifying.

Some of you may wonder why I moved back in with my wife and son. The answer is simple. I want to get rid of the ghost that lives here. I want to fight back at the thing that destroyed my family, and I'm going to win.

My brother and I tried to contact the spirit last night. I have been using recording equipment to try to pick up an EVP (Electronic Voice Phenomenon, for those of you not familiar), but so far, no luck.

The ghost is still present. You can feel it when you walk around inside. There is a certain heaviness that comes over you as soon as you cross through the door. Jake says he feels it too.

I don't know why the entity silent. I know it remembers us.

I won't give up. I will keep trying. And I will update you all here on my progress.

Please wish me luck.

KELLY SCROLLED, reading the next post.

MY BROTHER and I had our first success in provoking paranormal activity within the house. It first happened to Jake when

I was at work. He saw a crucifix thrown from the table into a pile of trash.

Later that night, instead of using recording equipment to capture the voice of the spirit, I used the crucifix to provoke a reaction. And a reaction we got! This thing, whatever is in our house, does not like religious objects. It ripped the cross from my hand and threw it against the wall, causing it to stick there by itself, upside down. When I tried again, it threw it onto the ceiling where I could not reach it.

Then, I brought down my old Bible, as a second test. It knocked it out of my hands and I watched as all the pages were ripped out and thrown all over the room.

The next day, Jake contacted a paranormal investigator who lives in town who is familiar with our house. He told Jake we were not dealing with a normal ghost, but rather something that has never been human. Something demonic. He has advised as soon as possible, but I won't give up that easily. This home is mine, and I will take it back by whatever means necessary.

"My goodness..." Kelly fingered the necklace at her throat as she read. The matter-of-fact way the entries were written frightened her. *And Jake was a witness to all of this?* She was still unsure if she believed any of it, but there was no way she would say that to Jake during such a fragile time for him.

The blog posts continued.

Ever since provoking the spirit with religious objects, paranormal activity has increased. And I'm afraid it has escalated too much.

It directly attacked my son, Daniel by writing vulgar words and drawing graphic pictures on his bedroom wall. Linda was furious, thinking Daniel did it, but I know better. The same thing happened when I was a boy.

The demon is up to its old tricks again.

Next, it lured Daniel to the tree house in the backyard at three o'clock in the morning. It used to happen to me as well, according to my brother, but I have no recollection of these episodes. Daniel doesn't remember climbing the tree either.

Thankfully, Jake was sleeping downstairs on the couch and could get Daniel away from the demon.

My family and I have moved out of the house and into a motel for the time being. Linda insisted that we go, and at first I argued, but now I think this is for the best.

I was wrong about this thing. I assumed it would attack me because it knew me, but no. It did not reveal itself to my parents back then — only to me and my brother. It has done the same and targeted my son Daniel, the most vulnerable one in the house.

And that cannot stand.

I am committed to removing this demon from the home. I will look into professional, religious help to achieve this. Unfortunately, there are not many paranormal or demonic experts around Rose Grove.

I may be forced to do this alone.

Please continue to pray for us.

THE NEXT DAY, after work, Kelly remained behind to grade papers, but she couldn't concentrate. Instead, she got back on the Internet and looked up Trevor's blog. There was no update.

Then, she opened a new tab and searched for Rose Grove, Georgia. There were many pictures of the quaint country town in the middle of spring, plus some articles geared toward tourists. The same newspaper article about Trevor buying the home also appeared. She scrolled past it.

The results faded into other keywords involving roses and groves. There simply wasn't much on the Internet about such a small place.

So Kelly refined her search.

She searched for *Rose Grove Georgia Haunted House.*

Funny enough, the first link was Trevor's website and blog. There was nothing else though.

Next, she tried. *Rose Grove History.*

The first page of results was about the history of the town and settlers who had founded it hundreds of years ago, but on the second page was something else that caught her eye. It was from a website dedicated to the "murderous history" of places around the country. Whoever ran the site had written a brief piece about Rose Grove.

When Kelly clicked on it, the first thing she saw was an old, black and white photo of the same house she had seen in the newspaper.

And beneath it was an article.

Rose Grove is an idyllic town two hours drive from Atlanta. If one were to visit, they would be treated with southern comfort food, feel-good vibes, and friendly locals.

But as with most pleasant places we've explored on the site, there is a little more to the story behind the charm. Many small towns have a secret history to bury, and Rose Grove is no different.

The Decker House is the largest and oldest house in town. Public records state that it was built in 1890 and has been a staple of the community ever since.

The house was commissioned by Thomas Decker, a wealthy banker who desired to live in a small, peaceful location. After construction was complete, Mr. Decker moved in with his family and young son, George, and remained there for about ten years.

The town sprang up around the house and Thomas Decker retired from his job and lived off his considerable wealth.

However, as time went on, it soon came to light that Thomas Decker was not the family man many believed him to be. One day, his son George showed up to the police station — bleeding, bruised, and with a broken arm. Although George was afraid to admit anything, the authorities figured he had been severely beaten by his father. The banker was arrested.

After this incident, Decker's wife left him and took their son away. By the time Decker was released from prison, he was all alone, and there was no hint as to where his wife had taken their son.

Decker grew unhinged. He came to believe everyone in Rose Grove knew where his son was, but refused to tell him. One day, he showed up drunk to the local bar and started a fight with a man named Benjamin Crow. Bystanders said Decker was out of his mind and accused Crow of having an affair with his wife and conspiring to hide her and his son away from him. The pair ended up in a fight which resulted in Decker bludgeoning Crow to death with a wooden chair.

Decker fled the scene, but the men in the bar pursued him back to his home. Before the police could arrive, the mob took justice into their own hands and lynched Decker from a large tree behind the house. Even after the authorities got there, no one was charged with a crime and Thomas Decker's body hung until it decomposed and withered.

As time wore on and the story of Thomas Decker faded from memory, few people have owned the house, and those that have don't live there for long. It is said that the ghost of Thomas Decker roams the halls of his home, chasing away inhabitants, still searching for his son that was taken from him.

KELLY LEANED BACK in her chair, wondering if Jake knew anything about the history of the house. Probably not.

Wasn't that how it worked? Didn't houses with dark histories attract bad energy?

But according to Trevor's blog, what they were dealing with wasn't a ghost at all. It was worse.

Something attracted to the negativity that bred within those walls for the last one hundred years.

25

1995

Dinner had become a silent affair.

Dad ate quickly and noisily, chewing with his mouth open and holding his fork wrong. If Jake or Trevor had done that, they'd be slapped on the wrist and told to mind their manners. Dad used to be so proper, too.

When he finished, he pushed his plate away, belched, and carried his beer to the living room, leaving the rest of the family to finish their food alone. Even though he was gone, no one spoke.

After dinner was over, Mom said, "Jake, can you help me wash the dishes, please?" Trevor smirked at him. Since his arm was in a cast, he was exempt from certain chores.

Jake didn't mind though. It gave him something to do and being close to Mom made him feel safe.

He stood on a chair at the sink. She washed and he dried, like a conveyor belt. Between each plate or fork,

Jake stole glances at his mother, wondering why she looked so sad. Probably because of his father and how mean he had become in the past couple months.

A wet plate slipped between Jake's fingers and landed on the kitchen floor. It shattered.

"Goddammit!" Dad shouted from the living room. "You want to eat off the table from now on?"

Mom closed her eyes and gripped the edge of the sink. It was a look that Jake knew well — one that meant she was upset but trying to calm herself and hold her tongue. Saying nothing, she retrieved the broom and dust pin from the pantry and swept up the broken shards.

"Sorry," Jake whispered.

"It's okay," Mom said. "I'll finish these. Why don't you go upstairs?"

Jake returned the chair he'd been standing on to the table. As he headed for the stairs, he glimpsed into the darkened living room. The only light came from the television screen, illuminating Dad in an ominous glow. He slouched out on the couch, a can of beer in his hand.

Something moved on the wall above Dad's head and Jake froze. At first it looked like someone was drawing with a marker. The lines connected and weaved together, forming a picture. Then the dark lines started to drip like blood.

Jake clenched his eyes closed for a second and then opened them. The bloody drawings took the shape of a monster that resembling a lion, with black eyes and a gaping mouth with razor sharp fangs. It appeared to stare right at Jake while Dad remained clueless inches from it.

"What the hell are you staring at?"

Jake had not noticed Dad looking at him. He raised a trembling finger and pointed at the wall.

"What?" Dad barked.

"Behind you," he managed, his voice catching in his dry throat.

Dad twisted around and looked at the bloody drawing, then back to Jake. "What are you pointing at? Just go to your room!"

"You can't see it?" Jake said, merely a whisper.

Dad pelted the can at Jake, who barely dodged it. It clanged on the dining room floor and beer spilled all over the tile. "Get the hell out of here!"

Jake sprinted up the stairs and into his bedroom, slamming the door behind him.

"What's going on?" Trevor asked.

But Jake knew it would be pointless to tell him anything. He only shook his head.

Downstairs, he heard his father shout for Mom to bring him another drink.

THE NEXT MORNING, Jake awoke to a loud crash and something breaking.

He shot up straight in bed, startled. Trevor did the same.

"Where the hell are my cufflinks!" Dad's voice boomed from his parents' bedroom. It was down the hall, and their door was always closed in the morning, which meant he was shouting very loudly.

Another crash. Jake and Trevor exchanged a glance. It sounded like he was tearing the room apart.

The door banged open and his heavy footsteps stomped outside their room. Jake's breath caught in his throat.

But he only directed his anger at Mom. "I have an important meeting today and you know I need to wear my lucky cufflinks! They belonged to my grandfather and if you can't find them I swear to God —"

"You're not the only one who's lost something," Mom shouted in a rare instance of fighting back. "I'm missing three necklaces and the earrings you gave me when you actually liked me!"

"Forget about those. These cufflinks have been in my family for generations. Find them before I get home today or I'll tear every room apart until they turn up."

"Quit shouting," Mom said. "You'll wake the boys."

"Lazy pricks need to stop sleeping all day, anyway."

Dad was right outside their door and Jake trembled, wondering when he would burst inside and accuse them of stealing his lucky cufflinks, then throw their things around in a rage.

Fortunately, he did not. He only stomped down the stairs and left the house.

"Did you take them?" Trevor asked.

"Are you kidding? No way! Did you?"

His brother only rolled his eyes.

Jake crept to the door and opened it a crack. Down the hall, he heard Mom sobbing and picking up the mess Dad had made.

Jake knew she'd spend the rest of the day looking for those cufflinks even though Dad was the one who probably lost them. It didn't matter. He always blamed others, always thought someone was stealing from him or trying to play a prank on him.

The afternoon wore on, and Jake turned out to be right. Although Mom didn't say anything or ask them about her missing jewelry or cufflinks, she still combed through the drawers in the kitchen, looked under each couch cushion, and even under the rug in the foyer.

"Wonder where they could be," Trevor said late in the afternoon. Mom was growing worried, checking her watch every five minutes. Dad would be home in a few hours.

"Should we help?" Jake asked.

"She's already searched everywhere," he whispered. "Where else could we look?"

"Yeah," Jake said. "Maybe you're right."

An hour later, Jake went upstairs to his bedroom and grabbed the comic book he was halfway through reading. When he did, something fell from between the pages and clattered to the floor.

There, at his feet, were Dad's two missing cufflinks.

Jake looked back and forth between the small orbs and the comic book in his hand. There was no way they could have ended up there on their own.

And if Trevor didn't do it, that meant their shadowy roommate did.

He picked them up and gripped them in his palm, the metal cold against his skin. He panicked, considering what to do with them.

That thing had been attempting to frame them. It had stolen the cufflinks because it knew it would make Dad angry. It had hidden them in their bedroom to get them in trouble. It was trying to sabotage them.

And if the cufflinks were in their room, that also meant…

Jake pocketed them and rummaged through his drawers, his closet, and under the piles of toys in the corner.

When he lifted his pillow, he found Mom's three missing necklaces, hidden almost in plain sight, but in such an absurd location that no one would have ever thought to check there.

Jake grabbed the jewelry. He checked over the landing to make sure the coast was clear and then snuck into Mom and Dad's bedroom. He placed the necklaces underneath their bed, but not completely hidden. It would look like they'd been dropped there. The cufflinks, however, he set on Dad's bedside table — a more obvious location.

The next time Mom went to her bedroom, Jake stood nearby and listened. He heard her sigh in relief when she found both items although it was clear she was confused — she knew she'd already checked everywhere a hundred times and didn't understand how she'd missed them.

When Dad came home, Mom gave him his cufflinks. He snatched them from her hand without a word of gratitude and slammed the bedroom door behind him.

Jake breathed a sigh of relief. That was the best outcome he could hope for.

Searching his room for stolen contraband became a regular activity for Jake. He reasoned that since the ghost's first plan to frame them had failed, it might try again. So he searched everywhere and under everything each morning, looking for anything that had been planted.

He wondered if he lay awake long enough at night if he would see the stolen objects floating into his bedroom and put in the hiding places. Staying up wasn't hard anymore — Jake found it difficult to get to sleep as the summer drew to its end. There were too many strange occurrences happening around the house, and they left in him a constant state of fear.

One night, Jake's eyes opened, and he was suddenly alert. The digital clock beside his bed told him it was three o'clock in the morning — a time he'd gotten used to. It was like his internal clock had somehow been set for it, and his eyes naturally opened on the dot.

He rolled over to begin the long process of trying to get back to sleep.

And saw the black shadow floating over Trevor's bed.

Jake's entire body seized. He tried to move, but he couldn't.

This is a dream.

The shadow was the same thing he'd seen in the tree house. It floated above Trevor's sleeping form, taking the shape of a person. The arm reached out to his brother, drifting, as if wanting to gingerly touch him.

Jake found control of his voice. "Trevor! Wake up!"

The figure's head snapped toward Jake, as if noticing him for the first time. Then several things fell from the ceiling on top of Jake, battering his head and body under the covers. It was too dark to identify what they were, but when they started to crawl, Jake threw off his blankets and leapt out of bed.

The moonlight through the window gave enough

light to see the dozens of cockroaches scurry around the room. They had appeared out of nowhere, raining down on Jake's head. He screamed as he brushed the remaining ones off his shoulders, shouting and crying.

Another ear-piercing scream bellowed behind him.

Trevor had woken up and was now face to face with the apparition. They were almost touching.

"Trevor!" Jake shouted.

Their bedroom door flew open, and the light turned on. In that instant, the ghost disappeared. So did all the cockroaches.

"What's wrong?" Mom said, tying her bathrobe.

"I saw the ghost!" Trevor pushed himself straight up in bed. Mom rushed to him and took him in her arms. "I swear! It was right above me!"

"Trevor, I think you had a bad dream."

"No!" Tears streamed down in his face. "I know what I saw. It was floating above me. It looked like a shadow."

"I saw it too," Jake said, taking the chance to get his story heard. He finally had another witness. "It was right on top of him."

Mom eyed Jake for a long time, and he found her tired expression hard to read. It was a look of stone.

"See!" Trevor pointed at him. "So we weren't dreaming. It was here, I swear!"

"Keep your voices down," Mom said. "Your father has work in the morning and you know he doesn't like to be woken up."

"I don't want to stay in here anymore." Trevor threw the covers off and squirmed out of Mom's embrace. He rushed to the door. "Come on, Jake, let's get out of here."

"It was really there, Mom," Jake pleaded. "Please believe us."

Mom said nothing. But, Jake noticed, she also didn't say she didn't believe them.

Has Mom seen it too? Does she already know what we're talking about? If she did, she didn't mention it.

They spent the rest of the night in the living room. Mom stayed up with them and the three of them played board games on the floor.

"It was black, and it was made of smoke and it felt like it wanted to kill me." Even as they played Monopoly, it did little to settle Trevor's nerves. Jake could tell he was thinking about the refrigerator magnets and how he hadn't been ready to admit the existence of a ghost quite yet, even though he'd seen them move on his own. Now, he had seen the entity with his own eyes. "I've never been so scared in my whole life."

"That's enough," Mom said. "You don't want your father to hear you say this stuff. He'll think you're making up stories."

"But I'm not. You believe me, right?"

Mom eyed him for a few moments. "Yes, Trevor. I believe you. Your move, Jake," she said, handing him the dice.

26

1995

Trevor was on edge for the next two days. Jake did not blame him.

"You really think that ghost is what makes me sleepwalk?" Trevor asked him with a shaky voice. "Is that how I ended up in the tree house that night?"

"Yeah."

"Why there, though?"

Jake only shrugged. He explained that the thing they'd seen in their room was the same entity Jake had seen in the tree house when he went to reclaim their comic books.

"I remember you were freaked out when you came back that night." Trevor chewed his lip. "What else happened?"

Jake began to tell him about the missing jewelry and cuff links, but the more Jake said, the more frightened

Trevor became, so he stopped talking about it altogether. For the first time in his life, it felt like he was the older one.

That afternoon, a truck pulled up in front of the house. It was purple and had a huge picture of an insect on the side, lying on its back, dead.

Mom greeted the exterminator at the door.

"You the lady who called about the cockroach infestation?" the man in the jumpsuit asked. Jake's ears perked up.

"Yes," Mom said. "I'm finding them everywhere."

"No problem. "I'll get rid of them for you. Give me a few hours."

"Any way you can make it quicker?" Mom chewed on her thumb.

"Hmm. Maybe. But a house this size... it'll take time. I'll do the best I can. Tell me when you want me to leave."

Mom nodded, and the exterminator got to work. First, he sprayed around the outside of the house and then came in and soaked the corners of the room with insecticide.

Jake understood what was going on. He remembered the cockroaches that fell on him from the ceiling the night he and Trevor had seen the apparition. But they had all disappeared at the same time as the ghost. They weren't really there.

Mom is seeing them too.

At four o'clock, Mom asked the exterminator to leave.

"Ma'am, I'm not quite done."

"Sorry, but you have to leave before my husband gets home." The exterminator raised an eyebrow. "I realize it's strange, but please. I'll still pay you full price." She dug cash from her purse.

"Ma'am, are you sure you've seen cockroaches?"

"Yes. Swarms of them. They pop up in the most random places too."

"Oh." He scratched his scalp underneath his cap.

"Why?"

"Well. I've been doing this a long time. And I know a cockroach infestation. You do not have one." Mom only stared at him. "Not saying you're not seeing them, but... there are no signs here you got an issue."

"I guess we're extra secure now that you've sprayed," Mom said. "Thank you for your time."

The exterminator gave Mom a strange glance. "No problem."

The purple truck drove away, and not five minutes later, Dad's car arrived in the driveway.

He walked in, silent and scowling, and trudged straight to the refrigerator for a beer. "What's that stench?" he asked Mom without looking at her.

"I don't smell anything," she said, voice thin.

Jake could detect the light scent of fresh pesticide all throughout the house.

Dad opened his beer and turned around, then spotted a piece of paper on the dining room table. The invoice left by the exterminator.

"Oh," Mom began, but it was too late.

"What the hell is this?"

"Harry..."

"One hundred dollars for the bug guy? What the hell are you thinking? We can't afford this right now." He slammed the beer onto the table, sloshing it all over the surface. Jake and Trevor ran upstairs to their room as the screaming escalated.

"Cockroach infestation? I haven't seen a single damn bug since we've moved in! Why don't you talk to me about stuff like this first?"

He berated her for a good ten minutes before it was over. He would be furious for the rest of the night, so Jake and Trevor found it best not to leave their bedroom until morning.

THE FOLLOWING EVENING, Dad left the house again soon after returning from work to head to the bar with some friends. Jake could only hope he returned home drunk enough to go straight to bed. If not, then he would be angry and seek to relieve some of that aggressive energy.

Jake found his mother in the backyard, watching the sun set over the trees behind their house. The sky was a light blue with smears of purple and orange. There was a small garden in the back, Mom's personal project to distract herself. It was a circular oasis of plants and decorations and a single bench. She sat on it, smoking a cigarette.

Jake had never seen his mother smoke before. It surprised him after all the times she pointed out people with cigarettes to him and Trevor, warning them to never do that, saying it would make them sick.

He crossed the backyard and went to her. When she spotted him, she made no effort to hide the cigarette. "Hey Jake. Everything okay?" He only shrugged. Mom patted the space next to her on the bench and he sat.

The fumes from the cigarette were strong and toxic,

making Jake want to cough. Mom stared ahead as she took a long drag, blowing the smoke through her thin lips. She looked tired and old, with large bags under her eyes and hair that hadn't been brushed that day. There was a bruise on her forearm in the shape of a hand where she'd been grabbed too rough.

"We should have never come here," Mom said after a long time.

"I know."

"Your father was never like this before. It's this house."

"Trevor wasn't lying the other night," Jake said. "There really was something in our room. It was floating over him, and it wasn't the first time I've seen it."

"I believe you." Mom took another drag of her cigarette.

"You do?"

"Yes. I've seen it too."

"Seriously?"

"It comes late at night when I can't sleep. It appears as a shadow in the corner of the room. It stands completely still and watches me. Even when I'm not looking at it, I know it's there. It makes me feel…"

"Very bad," Jake finished.

"Yes. As if it has a lot of sadness inside and it's able to transfer it directly to me." Mom tapped her heart to illustrate. "If it can make me feel like this, then I assume it's doing the same thing to your father. That is why his behavior has changed."

"Can we leave?"

"I've brought it up once," Mom said, and grimaced. "Never again."

Jake knew not to ask how that conversation had gone. "I don't want to live here anymore."

"Neither do I. But we have no choice. Money is a problem right now."

He was very sad when he looked at his mother. In a few short months, he had seen her transform from such a high-spirited woman to a shell of her former self.

"I'm supposed to be a good mom and tell you ghosts and monsters don't exist," she said. She took the last drag from her cigarette and stamped out the butt on the ground. She pulled out a pack and withdrew another, lighting it. The first puff of spoke caught the breeze and blew in Jake's face. "But I can't do that this time. There is something in this house, and it is evil. It wants to hurt us."

"So what can we do?" Jake asked.

Mom tapped the ashes off the end of her cigarette. "We need to get help."

"The cockroaches aren't real," Jake said, remembering the exterminator. "I've seen them too. They always disappear."

"That's not what I'm talking about. I mean serious help."

Jake wasn't sure what she meant by that, but it made him nervous. But if it would work, then he was willing to try anything.

Mom ran a hand through his hair and pulled him close to her. "Stay strong for me. I know you can. I have one more idea, and if that doesn't work, then I'll do what I must to make sure you and your brother are safe. We'll run away from here if we have to."

Jake gulped. He pictured them throwing suitcases into

the back of the car and escaping in the middle of the night. "If we did that, would Dad come too?"

Mom hesitated for a long time before she answered. "There's nothing in the world that could pry your father out of this precious house he loves so much. So I think it would just be the three of us for a little while."

27

1995

The final week of summer came with a huge surprise.

"Boys," Mom called.

Jake and Trevor looked at each other. They were in their room, trying to get through their summer reading for school at the last minute.

Each of them had become sensitive to being summoned by one of their parents. It usually meant they were in trouble.

At least this time, it wasn't Dad.

They found their mother in the foyer. Although it was nighttime, around eight o'clock, she was wearing a dress and her hair was down.

"Listen to me," she said. "We are about to receive a visitor." She crouched down and looked them in the eyes. "A man is coming to check the house. But here's the thing. Your father does not agree with me that he needs to be here, so he doesn't know. I waited for your father to work late. So please, boys, keep this a secret between us, okay?"

Trevor and Jake nodded.

Jake's curiosity burned.

The visitor arrived twenty minutes later. He looked to be about fifty, but Jake had always been bad at guessing the age of adults. He wore a denim jacket, jeans, and a white shirt and was accompanied by a pretty woman, blonde and maybe fifteen years younger than the man.

Jake and Trevor sat in the living room and observed from afar as Mom greeted the two.

"Thank you for coming. I apologize for the short notice," Mom told the man as they shook hands. "My husband… he doesn't think this kind of thing is real. And he would be furious if he knew I was doing this behind his back."

"I understand, ma'am," he said. "Arthur Briggs. This is Madeline."

The blonde woman did not bother to speak to Mom or introduce herself. Instead, she wandered into the living room, looking here and there as if she were searching for something.

And she looked very upset.

"Don't mind her," Mr. Briggs told Mom as she eyed the woman. "She's just doing her thing."

"What's going on?" Mom asked. She folded her arms over her chest as if she'd suddenly become freezing.

"Madeline is a clairvoyant," Mr. Briggs explained. "She senses things in the spiritual world more clearly than you and me. I often bring her along to situations like this because she is more in tune than I am and we can quickly figure out what we're dealing with."

Jake and Trevor exchanged a glance. They were talking about the ghost.

Jake suddenly had a heavy feeling of dread.

"Tell me," Mr. Briggs said, "What have you been experiencing?"

"Well." Mom looked visibly upset. She thumbed the necklace that hung around her neck. "There's been a lot of strange stuff going on since we moved into this house. Things have gone missing. Like my jewelry, or some of Harry's cufflinks. He thinks I'm stealing them and selling them, but that is ridiculous."

"Are you?" Mr. Briggs asked.

"No! Of course not!"

"Forgive me. But sometimes, with these cases, there is often a rational explanation, and we have to rule those out first."

Madeline returned. "There is definitely a presence here."

"What did you feel?" Mom asked.

"Before we get into that," said Mr. Briggs, "please finish telling me what you've been experiencing."

Mom took a deep breath. "The biggest thing of all is my husband. Harry is... different these days. He says and does things he has never done before. He's mean, rude, and... has started hitting the kids. We've spanked our children before, but... this is becoming too much." She began to cry.

Madeline put a comforting hand on Mom's shoulder.

"I'm sorry." Mom wiped her eyes with a tissue.

"Not to worry," Mr. Briggs said. "This is a normal occurrence in these situations. This entity that dwells in your house has a way to bring out negative emotions because it feeds on them."

"What does it want?"

"Do you believe in the supernatural, Mrs. Nolan?" Briggs asked.

Mom shrugged. "I guess I've always considered it was a possibility. And it's the only thing that can explain the weird stuff that's been going on around here."

"There is something in this house," Madeline said. "I sensed it as soon as I walked through the door."

"What does it want?" Mom asked again.

"It wants to inflict as much pain on your family as possible, and eventually destroy you," said Mr. Briggs.

Mom brought a hand to her mouth. She looked like she was about to start sobbing again.

"Here is what we can do," Mr. Briggs said. "It is called a binding ceremony. We'll walk throughout the house and order the spirit to leave. Although it is not from this world, it is compelled to listen to us if we command it, especially if we invoke the name of the Lord. After, I suggest you get a priest to bless the home. It shouldn't be able to remain after that."

Mom wiped her tears and nodded. "Please. Do anything you need to do."

Jake and Trevor watched from behind the door as Mr. Briggs sprinkled water into the four corners of the room. He said, "In the name of Jesus Christ, I command you to leave this place!"

Nothing happened.

Jake wondered if that worked.

Mr. Briggs seemed to think it would. Because after, he and Madeline went to the living room and did the same thing — water in the corners and Mr. Briggs shouting, "In the name of Jesus Christ, I command you to leave!"

The three moved from room to room, Mom only a spectator, uncertain and afraid. Trevor and Jake kept their distance in the shadows, looking on. From what Jake could gather, the rooms that Mr. Briggs had thrown the water in would no longer be a place where the ghost could be.

He wondered what it would do when it was cornered in the final room.

Mr. Briggs did Jake and Trevor's bedroom, and Jake let out an audible sigh of relief. He hoped it worked. Perhaps that would prevent Trevor from going into his trance at night.

When they got to Mom and Dad's room, Mr. Briggs asked, "Is this the only room left?"

"Yes." Mom said.

"Good. Let's get to it."

The front door opened and closed. Mom gasped.

Jake and Trevor hid at the other end of the hall, out of sight.

Heavy footsteps on the stairs, and then Dad appeared. He glared at Mom, Madeline, and Mr. Briggs. "Who the fuck are you?"

"Sir," Mr. Briggs began.

"What are you doing in my house?"

"Harry." Mom tried to keep her voice calm and gentle, but it trembled. "Please. Let me explain."

"Who the fuck are these people?"

But when Mom got close, Dad raised his hand, and she cowered away.

"There is an explanation," Mr. Briggs said.

"Get out of here!" Dad shouted.

But Mr. Briggs did not move. "Mr. Nolan, I understand you are upset. But if we can sit down and talk about this —"

Dad swung and punched Mr. Briggs right in the face. The man stumbled back against the wall. Madeline shrieked.

Mr. Briggs straightened himself, blood dripping from his lip. "Mr. Nolan — "

"If you won't get out, then I'll throw you out." Dad grabbed Mr. Briggs by the shirt and hurled him down the stairs. He fell hard and loud, ending up in a crumpled pile at the bottom.

"Harry!" Mom shouted. "Please stop!"

"Why are you letting strangers in my house?" He shouted back at Mom as he ran down the stairs. He kicked Mr. Briggs in the ribs and chest. He crawled toward the front door. Dad opened it and scooped Mr. Briggs up by the clothes and threw him onto the porch. Madeline ran past Dad and outside where she dropped to her knees to see if Mr. Briggs was okay. Dad slammed the door behind them.

Then he rounded on Mom.

"Please," Mom begged as Dad climbed the stairs. "He was only here to help."

"Help with what?" Dad spat. "If you tell me some fucking ghost story, I swear I'll kill you."

He grabbed her hard by the wrists and twisted them, forcing her to her knees.

Jake felt Trevor grab him by the arm and pull him into their bedroom where he closed the door.

Although they could still hear the slaps and Mom's sobs as Dad punished her.

Jake sat on his bed, knees up to his chest, crying as he listened to the horrible things just outside his door.

And when it was all over and Mom retreated to her bedroom and Dad downstairs to the television, Jake realized that after all that, Mr. Briggs had not completed the ritual.

28

2018

Jake returned home, every inch of his body feeling fatigued. At first he thought he was coming down with an illness, but there were no other symptoms — no cough, no fever, no congestion.

No, he was just weak. He had been deteriorating ever since he'd departed from Rose Grove.

He found Kelly on the couch, her laptop on her thighs. The look she gave him — he couldn't place it, but he hated it. Something between pity and concern. Maybe disgust?

"What?" he snapped.

"Are you okay?"

He clenched his fist. "How many times are you going to ask me that? I'm fine."

He wasn't, though. He'd spent the day watching Craig bounce around the office, delegating tasks that Jake knew he would do if he had gotten the promotion. He'd even had the nerve to come by Jake's cubicle and ask him to take on a client that was supposed to be an easy job — something he should give to one of the new guys. Jake remembered the flash of rage, the sudden desire to stand up and sock him in the nose. He'd barely resisted.

When the fury ebbed, he wondered where it had come from. He'd never felt so quick to anger and violence before.

"I'm worried about you," Kelly said. "Ever since…"

"I'm fine. You don't need to ask me anymore. Or better yet, just give Greg a call." The words spilled out of his mouth, and he had no idea why. But that was how he felt. Somehow, he knew Kelly was still in contact with him. Why wouldn't she be? Greg was much more handsome and successful than he was.

"What?" she asked.

"You heard me. Greg. Your ex who is better than me in every way. I'm sure you'd love to have him back."

"What are you saying?"

"Admit it," Jake said. His temper rose toward the tipping point. "You still talk to him behind my back, don't you?"

Kelly didn't respond.

"I knew it."

"He called once when you were in Georgia," Kelly said. "Only once. I talked to him for a few minutes before telling him not to call me anymore."

"Calling when I'm out of town," Jake said. "Figures. I suppose you expect me to believe the timing is just a coincidence?"

His mind filled with images of Kelly and Greg in bed, laughing at what an idiot he was for chasing a ghost while they got to spend their time together.

Maybe I ought to thank the demon, he thought. He hadn't had these realizations about her and Greg until he'd gone to Georgia.

"Jake," Kelly said, looking like she was ready to cry. She stood from the couch. "This isn't you."

"What does that even mean? I'm standing right here in front of you. I am me."

"You're not acting the same. It's — "

Something fell from the ceiling and landed on Jake's shoulder, then tumbled to the ground. A cockroach. Jake stepped away and watched it scurry into the kitchen.

The insect snapped him back into reality. He closed his eyes and took a deep, steadying breath.

The demon.

Its effect was far reaching and powerful. He should have known. *I need to be stronger than Dad. He gave in and didn't fight. This is what happened to him.*

"I think it's getting to me," he said, forcing his voice to calm.

"You must do something," Kelly said. "We can't go on like this."

"What can I do? I've already done a lot. Now look what's happening." His whole life was falling apart.

"I want to show you something," Kelly said. "Will you look?"

"What is it?" Jake asked, hesitant. He didn't know how much more of this he could take.

"Can you please just look? I don't know what to make of it but maybe you will."

Jake sat next to her on the couch and she passed the laptop to him. She'd found an article about the history of his childhood home and he read it.

"What do you think?" Kelly asked him.

"I've never heard this story before," he said. "It all makes perfect sense. They lynched him in the tree where we first experienced the demon."

"Maybe this explains why the house is like that," Kelly said. "Have you talked to your brother?"

Jake looked at her. "No. Why?" Kelly chewed her lip. "What do you know?"

She reached over and used the track pad to bring up another tab. Jake recognized his brother's paranormal website, the Spirit Seekers.

"He's been blogging," Kelly said. "I've been following along."

Jake read through the blog posts, terrified at what he might find.

At first, the posts were a recap of Jake's time spent at the house. Trevor must have written them while he was at work and none had any comments. There were few readers on his little corner of the Internet.

"Yeah," Jake said. "All of this happened. I witnessed it."

"My goodness," Kelly whispered. "Wait!" She brushed her fingers on the track pad. "There's more. I haven't seen these updates yet."

They read them together. Jake's gut clenched.

I WENT BACK to the house last night. The thing has trashed the place. Check out the pictures.

WHAT FOLLOWED WERE snapshots from inside Trevor's home. Giant holes gaped in the freshly painted living room walls, showing the wood and plaster behind them. The light fixture above the dining room dangled from the ceiling. The window on the front door had been smashed.

Then the photos grew more serious.

Daniel's bedroom walls were covered with horrible words, phrases and pictures. There was a crude sketch of a beheaded child, blood pouring from the neck. There were several naked women in lewd poses surrounded by upside down crosses that had been scribbled out.

The demon also left his signature, charming messages.

LITTLE DANIEL FUCKS GOATS

CHILDREN DESERVE TO BE IN HELL

The master bedroom was desecrated in much the same way.

LINDA IS A GIANT WHORE

FUCK YOU AND BURN IN HELL

Besides the messages, there were symbols scrawled on the wall that appeared to be from another world. The carpet had been torn up. The dresser had been toppled over and clothes were thrown everywhere.

"What on earth..." Kelly whispered.

"This is the worse I've ever seen it," Jake said. "It didn't even go this far when we were kids."

Jake scrolled. There was another blog post, dated one week later.

LINDA WAS VERY UPSET when she saw the state of the house. I don't blame her. She is now a believer and refuses to go back.

That means I had to clean up the mess on my own. I only go during the day because I refuse to stay in the house at night. That's when the activity begins again.

I threw away the broken furniture, rearranged the stuff that was still intact, swept up all the glass, turned the tables right side up. And I painted over all the horrible things written on the walls.

It was demoralizing having to do all the work since we've been renovating for three months already. The costs of the job are rising due to this little setback.

I have been reading up on the process of getting the house cleansed. Please continue to pray for my family during this difficult time.

THEN, four days later, Trevor posted again.

I HAVE BEEN SPENDING MORE time at the house, even going there at night. If I want to fight this thing, then I have to do it when it is most active. All the work I have done to fix up the house has been undone. As you can see, there is no point in cleaning up or continuing renovations until I defeat it. It will only keep destroying my home.

I begged the church to send someone to check it out, but they refuse. Apparently, the ceremony is not something that can be easily had. It requires approval from the Catholic church, and to get that, there needs to be a large amount of hard evidence. All I have are stories of my experiences, which are not sufficient, and these pictures, but they say anyone could have done that. They don't believe me. They think I'm crazy.

Maybe I am crazy. But I don't care. I will continue to fight. I will spend every night in the house if I must, praying and invoking the name of the Lord and commanding this thing to leave.

Please pray with me.

"Oh no," Jake whispered. "I told him not to go back there. I should have known he wouldn't listen."

Now that he'd seen the photos, Jake understood why he sensed the demon's increased presence in his own life. They had provoked it, and it was angrier than ever. It was going for the final blow, to finish destroying the Nolan family.

Its power was not bound by time or place. Its hand could touch Jake even hundreds of miles away, causing him to experience this sudden depression, fatigue, and anger. It was trying to wreck his job and destroy his relationship with Kelly.

"There's one more," she said.

The final blog post appeared at exactly three o'clock in the morning the night before.

Fuck this thing, whatever lives in my house.

It hates me, and I hate it back.

I am no longer afraid of it.

In fact, sometimes I spend entire nights here, just trying to piss it off

Ha ha ha

It can kiss my ass

It can fuck off

I will not leave until it goes first. Ha ha ha

Please continue to pray for my family. He he he he

THE WORDS GRIPPED Jake's heart in cold fear. He felt Kelly's hand on his arm, trying her best to comfort him.

"I have to go back," he heard himself say. "I thought he had a good handle on the situation when I left. But he's gone too far now."

"He needs you," Kelly said. She seemed genuinely afraid.

Jake opened a new tab and booked his flight to Atlanta.

29

The flight was uneventful, and as Jake waited for his luggage to appear on the baggage carousel, he took out his phone and called Linda.

The phone rang three times, then garbled, like the connection was poor. Jake hung up and tried again. Unfamiliar bags sprouted from the top of the machine and slid down the ramp onto the black conveyer belt.

It rang again, and this time it stopped ringing and fell into silence.

Strange. Maybe she was in a bad signal area or on the phone with someone else already.

Either way, he had to get in touch with her. He had to find out what Trevor was up to and if she and Daniel were okay.

Jake waited another minute and tried again. She answered.

"Hello?" came the familiar voice.

"Linda. Hi. It's me, Jake."

"Oh, hi Jake."

She seemed oddly pleasant. Jake would've thought she'd sound more distressed given the state of Trevor and her home.

"How are you?"

"I'm fine. And you?"

Fine? Really?

"Listen, I'm in Atlanta now and I'm about to rent a car and head to Rose Grove. How is Trevor? Is everyone safe?"

"Trev's fine, Jake. Everyone here is fine. No problem."

Jake paused. He spotted his bag on the belt, but let it ride past. "Linda. Are you sure?"

"Yes, Jake. Please don't bother yourself with us. We're fine here."

Jake said nothing for a long time. Neither did Linda. The line lingered on. A faint crackle threatened the integrity of the connection.

"Who are you?" Jake dropped his voice low so the surrounding people would not hear.

"What do you mean, Jake? It's me Linda. Your brother's wife."

"Fuck you!"

The next thing he heard was horrible, otherworldly laughter, a cackle straight from hell. Then the line went dead.

He needed to hurry. It would not let him contact anyone. The only way he would know the true state of the situation was to see it for himself.

Jake grabbed his bag and ran to the rental car desk. There, he booked a car and immediately set out on the familiar road to Rose Grove.

As the miles fell away underneath him, the lingering sense of dread became even more unbearable.

He turned off the main highway and onto the two-lane country road that would bring him back to town.

A few miles later, he slowed at a four way stop. The signal was red. Jake lingered there in the idling car, gazing out the window at the farmlands and empty fields that surrounded him. Contemplating what he was walking into. Wondering if he would walk out.

After five minutes, the light was still red.

Annoyed, Jake inched forward, hopefully to trigger a sensor. Nothing.

Then he realized what was going on.

Jake opened the car door and walked around the entire square intersection, looking up. All the lights were red at the same time, and not changing.

"Bastard," Jake muttered. He got back into the car and hit the gas, peeling out through the intersection, running the red light.

It knew he was coming. It would try to stop him.

Jake encountered three more intersections with signals. Although his was the only car, the light remained red. Jake gave each of them about a minute before he drove straight through it.

Twenty minutes outside town, having just passed the one and only road sign informing him that Rose Grove was dead ahead, he heard a loud pop.

The car swerved out of control. The high speed sent Jake all over the highway, kicking up black smoke and dust. His surroundings spun through the windshield as his car made circles down the highway. He gripped the steering wheel, his seatbelt locking and jabbing into his neck.

Then there was a loud crash and everything came to a sudden halt. Jake blinked several times and let out the breath he'd been holding. His heart hammered in his chest. His neck burned from the seatbelt stabbing into it and ached from the whiplash.

The passenger side was embedded into the thick trunk of a large tree. One of its branches fell and landed on the hood with a loud thump.

Jake struggled to unbuckle and climb from the car. He was too weak and dazed to stand, so he crawled through the smoke.

Black tire marks stained the highway, showing how badly he had spun out of control. There was not another soul around to have witnessed anything. He was alone in the middle of nowhere.

He lay on his back on the side of the road and stared at the sky, thankful to be alive. Knowing he had come very close to dying.

Knowing the demon had tried to kill him.

When he regained his strength, he stood and investigated the wreck. The car was totaled after hitting the tree. Both tires on the passenger side had blown at once.

Jake gritted his teeth. He knew this time they were playing for keeps. This thing was no longer simply trying to just scare him away.

It wanted to remove him from the equation. Permanently.

Jake forced open the crunched trunk and removed his bag. He slung it over his shoulder and proceeded to walk the rest of the way.

30

He reached Rose Grove at dusk. It was early evening, and the town was settling down.

Jake walked down Main Street, the familiar sights all around him. He limped from his car crash, his bag thrown over his shoulder.

His childhood home was a few miles away. By the time he arrived it would be dark.

But there was somewhere else he had to go first. It was a long shot, but it was a chance he had to take.

He'd looked up the address before he'd left. He found the house in a quiet neighborhood on the other side of Rose Grove, the section of town he never visited as a child, and that some people, he remembered, didn't consider part of Rose Grove proper.

The address turned out to be quite an old home; the siding was faded and flaking and the yard overgrown. It looked as if no one had lived there in a long time. Jake dropped his bag on the porch and knocked on the door, rattling it on its hinges.

He heard footsteps on the other side. The curtain drew back and in the darkness, Jake could barely make out the silhouette of a face in the window.

The curtain fell back into place, but the door did not open.

"Who are you?" came the voice from inside. He did not seem pleased.

"My name is Jake Nolan. I emailed you a few weeks ago, if you remember."

The man on the other side said nothing for a while. Then, "You knocked three times. Who are you really?"

Jake realized what was going on. He had not meant to knock three times, but now understood why the man was wary. "I really am Jake Nolan. I'm sorry. I didn't mean to scare you."

"What is your name?" the man asked.

"Jake Nolan!"

"In the name of Jesus Christ, I command you to tell me your name."

"Jake Nolan! And I need help. Please. My brother is in trouble."

The man inside was quiet for a long time. Then, the door unlocked and opened.

Arthur Briggs had aged although Jake remembered the face. His hair was gone, and he had a scraggly, grey beard. His eyes sunk into his skull, his frame thin and withered. He was dressed in slacks and nice button shirt.

Briggs looked Jake up and down, scrutinizing him, his gaze resting on his face for a few moments. "Ah, yes. I remember. You haven't changed much." He cleared his throat. "I don't think I can help you. I tried once before."

"It failed because of my father. Not because of you."

Briggs looked at him for a long time, reliving the memory. "Come in."

ARTHUR BRIGGS'S house was neat and tidy — a drastic difference from the exterior — and had a pleasant aroma coming from somewhere in the house. Perhaps incense or an air freshener.

"Coffee or tea?" Briggs offered.

"Coffee, please," Jake said. If things went his way, then they would most likely be in for a long night.

Briggs made the coffee while Jake took a seat in the living room. He tapped his hands on his thighs impatiently. In his gut, he knew time was ticking.

Trevor would not last much longer before completely breaking down.

Just like Mom and Dad.

When Briggs returned, he had two steaming cups. Jake accepted and took a sip. It was one of the best coffees he'd ever tasted.

Briggs sat in the chair across from him and crossed his legs. He studied him for a moment before speaking. "You've grown up."

"Yes," he said.

"I have grown old," Briggs said. "Now. What brings you here?"

"Because of the email you sent. You were right. This thing in the house... It is not human, and it wants to hurt us."

Briggs sipped his coffee. "Yes. By the sounds of things that's what you're dealing with. The provocation with the religious icons was a giveaway."

"What does it want?" Although Jake was sure he already knew the answer.

"It wants what the devil wants," Briggs said. "Chaos, destruction, murder, mayhem. And most importantly, to upset the plan of God and His Creation. To see everything burn."

"My girlfriend found an article about the history of the house." Briggs's brow perked up. Jake told him the story of the banker who'd been lynched in the tree in the backyard.

"I've never heard that story," Briggs said. He took a sip of coffee, thinking it over. "These demonic entities are not easily predictable, but at the same time, they can be. Not every location with a tragic history will attract a presence. And when the human and demonic cross paths, you never know who it will target."

"Children," Jake heard himself say.

"Beg your pardon?"

"This one targets children. First it was my brother, Trevor. Now it's my nephew, Daniel." He paused. "At least, it starts with children. It eventually started revealing itself to my mother, too."

"I see. It sounds to me that it is doing what demonic entities do," Briggs said. "It will linger dormant at first, but begin to think of the place as its own home, its own property. When your family moved in all that time ago, it did not like it. If you were dealing with a ghost — a spirit of someone that was once human — then it would be a different story. A ghost would just be confused, unsure why strangers have come into his house. And he would simply need reminding that he is dead so he could move on, and then you wouldn't be bothered anymore.

"But this thing... not this. It has other desires. It is glad you came because now it has victims and will choose the most vulnerable to attack. As you said, children are common targets. It incites fear, because once there is fear, you will start to lose control. You will doubt the things you see are real. Maybe you will think you've gone crazy. The victims slowly become unhinged. Once that happens, they then do terrible things they have never dreamed of doing before. Carrying out the demonic's plan."

Jake remembered everything that had happened to his family before. His father slipped into alcoholism and abuse. His mother, once strong and proud, became broken around the man she had once loved and eventually swallowed a handful of pills. Jake and Trevor, innocent and afraid and scared, had been framed by the demon for things they did not do so they would get in trouble and beaten, leaving scars on their psyches that would never heal.

And it had worked. Jake learned that he could not confide in his parents, to always look over his shoulder for the next thing that the spirit had done that he would be blamed for.

And how over time, all of those things had splintered the Nolans. Ruined them. Led to the early deaths of both Mom and Dad, and left his relationship with his brother broken.

And now it was trying to do the same with Trevor and his family.

"It is still there," Jake said. "And my brother is on his last leg. We need help."

Arthur Briggs's face fell. He looked down into his coffee, thumbing the handle, thinking. Then, he said, "I cannot assist you."

"You're the only person who can. No one else in this town believes. You came to help before, but it was cut short. What if you had completed the ritual you were doing?"

"The binding," Briggs corrected.

"Right. The binding. If that had finished, would things have been different for me? Would I still have a family?"

The demon had used Dad to stop the ceremony prematurely, and the demonic presence remained.

"Hard to say," said Briggs.

"I'm begging you," Jake said. "My brother has moved back into that house and he's trying to fight it on its own. But he doesn't know how to do what you do. He doesn't have the experience. I think he demon is already taking over him. Controlling him. The cycle is repeating."

"I gave this all up a long time ago," Briggs said. "It is a dangerous and exhausting ordeal and my body cannot handle it anymore. At every binding I ever did, I have been attacked, beaten, scratched, cut, and thrown. These things will fight back. When I was a young man, I could take it. But now, it would kill me."

Jake knew what it was like to be tossed from the tree by the demon. To be sent into a spiraling car crash.

"What can I do?" Jake begged, setting the coffee cup aside. "Please, Mr. Briggs. If we do not stop this thing tonight, then another family will be destroyed by this spirit. I tried to save my brother on my own because that's how I learned to deal with this when I was a kid. I learned no one would ever believe me and that I was alone. No one can win if they attempt this by themselves. My brother is trying, and he is dying. You know this. So please. I'm begging you."

Although the room was dim, Jake could see the look on Briggs's face — a mixture of pity, doubt, and above all else, fear.

Briggs sat his cup aside and sighed. "Okay, this one time. But just so you are aware, if this doesn't work — and it is common for the binding to fail — I cannot do it again. Your brother must move out of the house."

"I promise," Jake said.

"I will spend tomorrow morning preparing. Gather some supplies. Come back around two and we can get started."

Jake's hope crashed. "Tomorrow? That's too late. We have to go now."

Briggs frowned. "We shouldn't confront the demonic at night. That is when it is most active and violent. It is like fighting an enemy on their home turf."

"Mr. Briggs, my brother won't last another day in that house."

Briggs chewed his lip and furrowed his brow. Jake understood why Briggs wanted to fight during the day, but they simply didn't have enough time.

"Fine," Briggs said. "We will go tonight. But listen and understand. You must be very diligent. Very aware. And always do exactly what I say when I say it. Is that clear?"

"Yes," Jake said, nodding.

"Very well. Let me gather my things. Then we can go."

31

Arthur Briggs drove an old truck that looked like it could barely run. Jake rode shotgun as it lumbered along. The two men were silent. Before they left, Briggs had grabbed a leather satchel and slung it over his shoulder. Jake didn't ask what was inside. Gear? Supplies? Who knew?

Briggs needed no instructions on how to get to there. He went straight there, and the monstrosity loomed against the darkened sky. All the lights were out and the entire house was quiet.

There was a single car in the driveway — Trevor's. When Jake got out of the truck, he saw that the front hood was up and the cables were ripped out of place. It would never run.

"Shit," Jake muttered, thinking about the destruction to his rental.

Briggs glowered down at the tangled mess of wires. "He's trapped here."

"I can sense it already," Jake said, turning his gaze to

the house. "Same thing from all those years ago, except it's heavier now. Angrier. It knows the fight is real this time."

Dread swirled in Jake's chest, the familiar crushing weight that came over him when he was in the demon's presence. He closed his eyes and tried to will himself to push forward.

Jake led the way toward the house. He climbed the porch steps — and was immediately knocked back by a tremendous force, sharp pain jolting through his chest. He stumbled backwards. Something warm dripped down his skin underneath his shirt.

There were three scratches above his heart — like a bear's claw. Blood had stained the front of his shirt.

Briggs stared at the wound, his face stony and unmoving, as if nothing out of the ordinary had happened. "I have a few scars myself. If we make it out of this, remind me to show you."

Jake pushed the pain from his mind and climbed the steps once again, wary and hesitant, as if waiting to step into a trap. He wondered if he would be attacked again if he got too close. But he made it to the front door and Jake couldn't help but wonder if the demon was inviting him in. Wanted him to enter its house full of horrors.

Jake jiggled the knob, but it did not move. So he stood back and kicked the door in with as much force as he could muster. The old frame splintered and the door flew open, banging against the wall behind it.

Inside, everything was silent and dark.

Jake went for the lights, but the power was out. Figured. The thing liked the darkness. Needed it.

"Trevor?" Jake shouted. He took a few steps in and peered into the living room. The furniture was in complete disarray and destroyed as the pictures on the website had shown. To his right the dining room was also trashed, with blasphemies, smut, and mysterious symbols painted on the walls. The house had become a shrine from hell.

"Trevor, where are you?"

Jake caught sight of something at the top of the stairs.

A figure standing in the darkness. A shadow.

It descended toward him. Then it ran.

Trevor raised his arm, a knife gripped in his hand. He shrieked as he charged his brother, weapon raised, ready to strike. Jake froze in place, unable to look away from the insane, raging expression in his brother's wide eyes.

Briggs grabbed Jake and pulled him to the side at the last moment. Trevor ran right past and out onto the porch before he could slow himself.

Jake whirled around and pounced on his brother, knocking him down to the ground, sending the knife spiraling away.

Trevor was unrecognizable. In the past two weeks, he had lost a ton of weight, probably having not eaten at all. His skin was wrinkled and pale, his eyes wild and crazy. There was no hair left on his head at all. He looked ten years older.

Now, his brother glared at him like a madman, struggling against him, trying to push him off, but his body had grown too weak. Jake had him pinned to the ground.

"Trevor! It's me, Jake!"

Upon hearing his name, Trevor calmed. His eyes softened, came back to Earth, and he truly saw his brother for the first time.

And then he wept.

Jake sat aside and cradled his brother's head in his lap, stroking his back like a child.

"It's okay, Trev. I'm here. I will get rid of this thing for you."

"Jake," he whispered. "You can't go in there. Please don't."

"We have to. We need to finish what we started twenty years ago."

"No. I was wrong and you were right. We should leave. Run away, burn the house down. Forget all about it." His voice trembled and tears streamed from the corners of his eyes. "We need to put it in the past."

They were words Jake had wished he'd heard weeks ago.

But he knew Trevor had been more right than he realized. The thing had followed Jake home, affecting his life, driving his stability into the ground. No, Trevor was the one who'd been correct. The demonic entity had to be dealt with. Until it was, it would never let up, never let them go.

"We should begin," Briggs said sternly.

"Trevor," Jake said. "Stay out here. When we finish, we will come for you."

Trevor nodded. He wiped at his nose with the back of his hand.

Jake and Briggs went inside, the heavy, oppressive feeling returning to the pit of Jake's stomach. The temperature was unnaturally cold and Jake could see his breath frost in front of his mouth when he breathed.

He followed Briggs into the living room where he lowered his satchel to the floor and pulled out a large flashlight. It shone bright through the darkness, piercing the black away. He handed a second one to Jake.

"The process is called binding," Briggs said. "We will progress through each room and command the spirit to leave. If we invoke the name of the Lord, it is compelled to obey. As you remember, we got through most of the house twenty years ago, but your father came home and disrupted the ritual. My guess is that was no coincidence, but rather by design."

"I think so too," Jake said.

Briggs rummaged through his bag and pulled out a small vial. "Holy water. My last bit from my days in the field."

Jake shined his light around the room. The place was a mess. There was trash everywhere, and a rotten stench emanated through the air. Black paint had been splattered on the forest green walls and the light fixture above had been ripped from the ceiling and was now dangling by wires a few inches from the ground.

"It's a miracle your brother is still alive," Briggs said. "The thing has taken its toll on him. And anyone who came through the door would also be in danger as you saw. Imagine if his wife had tried to come here."

Jake winced. He wondered where Linda was and if she was okay.

Something caught Jake's eye. On the coffee table was a cardboard box filled with familiar objects and sprang up dread in his heart.

Alphabet refrigerator magnets.

"Oh no," he muttered.

"What are these for?" Briggs asked. He picked up an H and examined it before dropping it back into the box.

"These toys got us in a lot of trouble when we were children. The spirit would arrange them on the refrigerator in bad words that would get us beaten by Dad."

"Your brother brought some back in the house."

"He was using them to talk to it," Jake said.

Briggs's face turned grim. "No matter what, under no circumstances, should you ever communicate with it." It looked like Trevor had bought many packs of the letters — the large box was filled to the top.

"Trevor doesn't agree."

The box tipped over by itself. The letters scattered on the hardwood floor around their feet.

Then they flew toward the wall.

UNDER NO CIRCUMSTANCES SHOULD YOU FUCK YOUR MOTHER HA HA HA

"We will not listen to you," Briggs said. "You cannot harm us!"

A picture frame — one of the last still mounted on the wall — dislodged and flew toward Briggs. He ducked. It crashed into the corner, shattering into pieces and leaving a hole in the plaster.

No wonder Briggs thought he was too old for the job.

The letters fell away and new ones replaced themselves the wall.

KELLY STILL FUCKS GREG HA HA HA

. . .

JAKE WINCED. *It's true. There's no avoiding it.*

Anger built inside him, flashing faster than he thought possible. Maybe the reason he was so miserable around the house was not because of a demon, but because he was living with an unfaithful —

"Don't listen to it," Briggs said. "It will say anything to stop us. To make us weak."

Jake caught his thoughts and wrested back control. He took a few steadying breaths, frightened by how the demon knew which of his buttons to press.

The letters fell, then were replaced.

I KILLED YOUR DAD HA HHU HU HU

THEY DROPPED. Then more.

YOUR MOM KILLED HERSELF SHE WAS A SLUT SHE LET ME FUCK HER HA HA HA

JAKE TURNED AWAY from the wall. New messages continued to write themselves, but Jake refused to read.

"That's right," Briggs said. "Ignore it." Briggs went to the corner of the room and threw some of the holy water. He repeated the same thing in all four corners.

Jake's resolve broke, and he peeked.

I WILL KILL TREVOR TOO HA HA

. . .

TREVOR LIKES TO TOUCH BOYS EVEN LITTLE DANIEL

"In the name of the Lord Jesus Christ, I command you to leave this place!" Briggs shouted.

The letters fell to the floor. The room was silent and still and they were alone again.

"Is that it?" Jake asked.

"No," Briggs said. "It has only left this room. We must continue."

Next was the entrance foyer.

Three knocks rapped on the front door. At first, Jake thought it was Trevor. Then he remembered to count the knocks.

"Ignore," Briggs said. He tossed holy water around the room. His arms moved in jerks, slinging a few sprinkles here and there. "In the name of the Lord Jesus Christ, I command you to leave this place!" He shouted even louder.

Next was the dining room. There was hardly any space to walk inside. The dinner table had been smashed to pieces — something that would have taken a tremendous strength. Paint cans were strewn around, their colors mixed and splashed on the walls and floor. The plastic tarp was torn to shreds. Many of the plates from the kitchen had been thrown and shattered. Forks and knives were also on the floor, deadly points lying like silent traps.

Briggs threw his water at the corners. "In the name of the Lord Jesus Christ I —"

A big steak knife among the silverware shot up and whirled, blade over handle, toward Jake. He jumped out of the way just in time, before it embedded itself deep into the wall. It had been aimed right at his heart.

"I command you to leave this place!" Briggs finished. He seemed unaffected by Jake's near death experience.

All was silent.

Next was the kitchen.

There, heavy footsteps clomped on the ceiling above them. It sounded like a ten ton man was stomping around in boots made of iron, trying to pound his way through the roof. Tiny bits of plaster sprinkled down on their heads.

"It cannot scare us away," Briggs whispered as he threw the holy water into the four corners of the room. "It is retreating to the second floor. In the name of the Lord Jesus Christ, I command you to leave this place!"

Silence fell in the kitchen.

Now, all that remained was upstairs.

They climbed the stairs, Jake gripping the handrail. He read the painted messages on the walls.

LITTLE DANIEL LIKES TO BE FUCKED

LINDA HAS A FAT CUNT HA HA HA

AT THE TOP, the landing was filled with clothes from the bedrooms. They had been ripped and trampled.

Then, something pushed Briggs. His arms flailed as he

tried to catch his balance. He flew backwards into the railing, which gave way and broke behind him. Jake reached out and grabbed the edge of his jacket at the last second. His weight almost took Jake tumbling overboard with him, but Jake managed just enough strength to pull him back, and they both fell to the floor.

Briggs struggled to straighten himself and propped himself against the wall. He rubbed his sternum, grimacing in pain. "Bastard is strong."

"You're telling me," Jake said, standing. He checked the scratch wounds on his chest. They burned with fiery pain and his shirt was soaked through with blood.

Jake helped Briggs to his feet. He wasted no time in throwing the holy water into the four corners of the hallway. "In the name of the Lord Jesus Christ, I command you to leave this place!"

Next was the master bedroom.

The bed was flipped on its side and the television was smashed to pieces. Upside down crucifixes of all shapes and sizes covered the walls. The temperature was freezing, colder than anywhere else in the house.

"Final room," Briggs said. This was how far they had come before when Dad had interrupted the last binding ritual.

Briggs examined his vial of holy water with the flashlight. Only a little remained in the bottom of the glass.

"Let's do it," Jake said. He felt eyes on him, seeming to come from all over the place, staring at him. Glaring at him.

They were not alone. The presence of the demon was stronger than he had ever felt before.

Because it lingered only in the master bedroom now.

It's only remaining refuge.

Which meant it was angry. Desperate.

Briggs sprinkled the holy water into the corners one at a time. "In the name of —"

A large dresser moved from against the wall by itself, whirling at the man with surprising speed.

"Look out!" Jake shouted.

He was not quick enough. It crashed into Briggs, the plywood splintering as if it had been hit by a wrecking ball. The old man spiraled backwards, landing hard on his back, the vial of holy water falling from his hand.

Blood dripped from cuts on his face, lip, and nose. He lay limp, his body writhing in pain. Jake knew from the force of the impact that something was surely broken. Maybe many things.

Jake dropped to his knees and leaned over the old man. "Briggs! Come on, you need to get up!"

Briggs shook his head. "I… can't."

The walls of the room trembled. There was a voice — deep, dark, and otherworldly. At first it was distant, but then grew louder and clearer. It was laughter.

The wall above the flipped bed was blank, devoid of any scribbled vulgarities or damage. There, something appeared. Jake watched as dark lines manifested themselves, connecting like pieces of art coming together on their own.

It became the face of a horrible creature, one that could be straight from hell. The eyes were black, the head shaped like a lion. The mouth was open and gaping, with razor sharp teeth. On either side of the face were claws, each with fingernails resembling giant scythes.

The image was not moving, as if painted there. But

Jake got the impression it was very much alive. It could see them, hear them. The laughter grew louder.

"Come on," Jake said. He placed his arms underneath Briggs's knees and neck, preparing to lift him. He had to get the old man out of there.

"No!" Briggs managed. "F-f-finish!"

"What?"

Briggs looked up at him with wide eyes filled with fear. His dropped flashlight made his face whitewashed and bright. "Finish!"

Jake knew what he had to do. He searched the floor around him for the vial of holy water, unable find it in the debris.

The demon's laughter became louder in Jake's head. Echoing there, making him cover his ears with his hands to block it out. But it was inside, crippling and weakening him, and he couldn't even move.

The standing mirror on the other side of the room shattered, but the glass did not fall to the floor — it flew supernaturally straight at Jake. The shards zipped right past him, the tiny sharp bits cutting his face, hands, and clothes, drawing new blood.

When the glass had passed him, Jake looked up into the face of his enemy. The eyes had dripped. The creature had been manifested in blood.

Jake collapsed to his knees. The laughter was too much. Being so close to the demon made him feel like his soul was being sucked away. And he wanted to give up, to let it take him.

My job is gone. Kelly doesn't love me.

Nothing mattered anymore. What was it all for?

That's right, said a deep voice in his head. *I have saved you from a false life. You owe it all to me.*

The demon was correct. Jake would never know about his boss's disloyalty or Kelly's true feelings without it. It understood more about his life than he did.

Jake knew it was over. He wished for relief, craved to submit fully to the entity inside the house. *Just take me. Get this over with. Make the pain stop.*

Then someone grabbed his shirt and pulled him to his feet. And when Jake opened his eyes, he saw his brother.

And in his hand, he held the vial — last of the holy water.

"Jake," Trevor said, eyes wide and desperate.

The world around Jake became clear again. The terrible thoughts fell from his mind, and Jake realized that once again, they had been put there by the demon.

And he knew what he had to do.

He wound back like a pitcher on the mound and launched the vial at the wall. It shattered against the face of the creature, and the voices and laughter inside of Jake's head ceased.

Jake found his last piece of strength remaining. "In the name of Jesus Christ, I command you to leave!"

Just as the blood had appeared out of nowhere, it dematerialized. As it did, the weight on Jake's body lessened and the temperature of the room began to rise.

Soon, the blood on the wall was completely gone as if never having been there. For the first time ever, being inside the old house felt… normal.

Trevor and Jake looked all around, waiting for the next attack, but nothing came. And nothing would come.

The two brothers embraced, holding each other for a long time.

32

Jake and Trevor supported Arthur, his arms around each of their shoulders, and helped him down the stairs. He winced the entire way down.

Once outside, they brought him to his truck, where they dropped the tailgate and let him sit.

"What's happening?" he asked, dazed and sweaty from the painful walk from the bedroom. "Is it over?"

And just then, the refreshing peace that had overcome them inside the house disappeared. The same dreadful, heavy feeling returned, the one that Jake had become accustomed to.

It hit the three men at the same time. Jake and Trevor exchanged a worried glance.

"It's still here," Trevor said. "It didn't work."

"We must have missed a room," Briggs said.

Jake understood. "No, not a room. Wait here." He opened Briggs's satchel and removed a wooden crucifix. Then he started walking.

"Where are you going?" Trevor shouted after him, but Jake did not answer.

He went around to the backyard. The cloudy night left everything plunged in darkness. Jake heard Trevor's footsteps scurrying behind him, trying to catch up.

The silhouette of the big tree loomed above them. And Jake sensed the demon's presence stronger than ever. "The one last place it can go," Jake said.

"What do we do now?" Trevor asked.

Movement from the old tree house.

A figure fell from the branch, but before it hit the ground, was caught and suspended in the air. Dangling. Swaying back and forth.

Someone hanging from a noose.

"What the hell?" Trevor took a step backward behind Jake.

"It isn't real." Jake was confident in that. He knew this thing's tricks now. "You aren't real!" Jake shouted at the hanging form.

As soon as the words left his mouth, the body fell from the tree as if the rope had been cut. Before hitting the ground, its fall slowed, then stopped, floating a few inches above the grass. The figure had no legs — the lower half trailed into a plume of black smoke.

And it hovered toward them.

"Jake," Trevor said, stepping backwards.

But Jake did not budge.

As the form neared, Jake saw it had taken the shape of a man wearing a black suit, one from a hundred years ago. The head hung loose, facing the ground. Then it snapped up, the lynched neck at a grotesque angle, the noose still wrapped taut around it.

The eyes glowed bright white. The face, although resembling a human, had a mouth that was much too large. It fell open, revealing jagged teeth and a black tongue.

A voice emanated from the figure — not coming from the mouth, but resounding inside Jake's head.

I killed your family. They all belong to me in hell!

"Enough!" Jake shouted.

If he could remove the demon from the house, he could remove it from the place where it originated.

The demon raised its hand, ready to attack. The arm was human enough, but the hand split into a large claw with three long fingers sharp as scythes.

And Jake held the cross up in front of him, arm outstretched.

The demon froze where it was.

"In the name of Jesus Christ, I command you to leave!"

The demon floated backwards, its face twisting in agony and rage at the words coming from Jake's mouth. As if they physically pained it.

"In the name of Jesus Christ, I command you to leave!"

Fuck you! Your God doesn't care about you! He gave your family to me! But even as it projected its cruel voice, it fell backwards, losing ground. And it had nowhere else to retreat to.

"For the third and final time," Jake shouted, "in the name of Jesus Christ, I command you to leave!"

The demon's human form burst into a cloud of black smoke that drifted underneath the tree house where the body had hung. Then it seeped into the earth as if being sucked in.

The peaceful relief returned. It felt as if the gravity all around Jake had suddenly become lighter.

"The tree," Trevor said. "The one last place it had to run to."

"And now it's gone," Jake said. And then he remembered the story he'd read about the history of the house. About why the tree was the last place the demon could hide. "Thomas Decker," he muttered.

"Who?" Trevor looked at him, confused.

"Thomas Decker," Jake said, louder as the idea came to him. "Do you have a shovel?"

"Yeah. In the old shed around the other side of the house."

Jake went to the white sheet metal structure. Inside, he used the flashlight on his phone and found what he was looking for.

"What are you doing?" Trevor asked when he returned.

"I have a hunch." He broke ground in the exact spot where the demon had retreated after being forced to leave. A patch of land directly underneath the tree house.

Trevor held the phone flashlight while Jake worked. Sweat seeped from his skin in the warm night, beads of perspiration dripping off the end of his nose.

"We need to get Briggs to a hospital," Trevor said.

"We will," Jake said. "But first…"

And then his next shovelful of dirt unearthed something horrifying, but expected.

The yellowed bones stuck out of the dirt. Jake scraped the shovel over the top of the shallow grave, revealing even more. Ribs, vertebrae, and a rounded, human skull, the mandible hanging open as if screaming.

"What in the world..." Trevor shined the light around the remains. "How did you know?"

"Thomas Decker," Jake said. "The first owner of this house." He glanced up at the tree branch overhead and remembered what had taken place there a hundred years before.

Jake stuck the shovel in the ground and leaned on it. He'd sweated through his shirt and the effort had brought new pain to the bloody cuts on his chest. "We'll call the police to do the rest. With these bones gone, and the demon banished, everything should go back to normal." Trevor still looked confused. "Come on. I'll tell you all about it on the way to the hospital."

33

An hour later, in the emergency room, Briggs was diagnosed with three broken ribs, a fractured forearm, and a shattered nose. He was put into a cast.

Jake needed stitches on the three claw marks on his chest and got bandages for the tiny cuts from the mirror shards.

The doctor, as he worked, asked Jake where the wounds had come from and Jake old him that a dog had scratched him. The doctor clearly knew that was a lie, but didn't press it.

As he watched the man stitch him up, he knew those marks would be on him for the rest of his life. Scars to remind him of the demon that had haunted him for the past twenty years.

Linda and Daniel joined them at the emergency room. But Linda did not rush to her husband's side, but to Jake's. "Is he safe? Is he better?" She had also lost weight, and her face was marked with fear.

Jake saw how afraid of Trevor Linda had become. "Yes," he said. "He's better now."

Only then did she go to her husband and embrace him. Jake watched the family from afar on the other side of the emergency room, reuniting in peace for the first time in a long while.

And Jake knew it was truly over.

ONCE JAKE WAS DISCHARGED, he and Trevor stood in the parking lot while Linda and Daniel continued on to the car.

"You look like hell," Jake told him. Although he'd come back from the slight insanity that had taken over him, the physical effects still showed on his body. "You need a cheeseburger. And a toupée."

"You don't look too good yourself," Trevor said, chuckling. A short silence fell between them before Trevor spoke again. "Thank you for coming back. If you hadn't… "

"Good thing you've been updating the blog," Jake said.

"I couldn't have done this without you. And maybe you were right. I probably shouldn't have attempted it at all."

"I think you were the one who was right," Jake said. "This had to be dealt with. No matter how much I tried to block it out, it still affected me." He shuddered when he thought of the damage to his career and his relationship with Kelly. He couldn't wait to get home so he could correct things in both areas.

"Either way, it's gone," Trevor said.

"Yeah."

"And I'm sorry for how I treated you at my wedding. And for everything the past couple of years. I shouldn't have been so isolated."

"Hey. It's all behind us." And he meant it.

"What will you do now?"

"Go home, I guess," Jake said. He wanted to tell Trevor how the effects of the demon had followed him to Texas, but decided against it. It didn't matter anymore, and he would be quite happy to never bring it up again.

"Let's…" Trevor rubbed the back of his bald head. "Let's try not to let too much time pass. You know, before we see each other again."

"Sure," Jake said. He held out his hand, and Trevor shook it.

Then Trevor pulled him into a massive bear hug.

The two brothers embraced each other in the hospital parking lot. Trevor squeezed him hard, hurting his bandaged cuts and stitches, but Jake didn't mind.

JAKE BOARDED the first flight he could back to Houston. When he arrived at the airport, it was four o'clock in the morning. Instead of waking Kelly up to come and get him, he took a taxi.

He was home by five. When he walked into the living room and dropped his small suitcase, Kelly emerged from the bedroom, wrapping her robe around herself.

"Hey," Jake said.

"Hi." Her voice groggy from sleep. "You didn't tell me you were coming home. I would have picked you up."

"Not in the middle of the night," Jake said. He went and took her in his arms. Her body was rigid and unsure. He kissed her, but she still seemed distant.

"What happened?" Kelly said, feeling the bandages underneath his shirt. She lifted it up and gasped when she saw the white dressings on his skin. "Oh my God."

"It's okay. I'm fine."

"No you're not. What are these, cuts?"

"Yes. But the doctor stitched them up."

"Who did this to you?" she asked.

Jake did not respond, and Kelly seemed to figure out the answer herself.

"Is it…"

"Yes," Jake said. "It's over."

"You're sure?"

"Definitely."

She searched his eyes for a long time, and then put her arms around his neck and pulled him into a tight hug. "I didn't fully understand what was going on," she whispered. "But I didn't like it."

"I'm sorry for the way it made me act. And the things it made me do. I should have been stronger."

"You were under a lot of pressure," Kelly said. "With your brother and all."

"I'll tell you everything in the morning," Jake said. "No more secrets. It doesn't matter anymore. All is resolved." Already he felt better about his past knowing the demon was back in hell where it belonged.

"You don't have to," she said.

"I want to. You have a right to know."

She kissed him again, and they went to bed together. There, Jake slept soundly for the first time in weeks.

One month later, Trevor and Linda invited Jake and Kelly for a visit during the holidays. Once Christmas vacation arrived, they packed their bags and traveled to Rose Grove, where Jake introduced his girlfriend to his childhood town and home. And, during the long drive there, told her everything that had happened to him and Trevor in their youths, and why the family had been destroyed. It felt cathartic to finally get it off his chest, and Jake realized it was silly to have not done so sooner.

When they arrived, Jake hesitated. The mental scars remained, and they kept him from approaching the house.

"You okay?" Kelly asked.

"Yeah," he said. "It's just strange."

But when Trevor and Linda came out on the front porch to greet them, all Jake saw was a normal and healthy family.

And when Jake went inside, he sensed none of the old dread that used to overcome him from simply walking in the door.

It was over.

The hate and despair were gone and the trauma of the house's past had been erased, returned to the history books where it belonged.

The only thing left was love and a happy family.

NEVER MISS A NEW RELEASE AND GET A FREE NOVELLA!

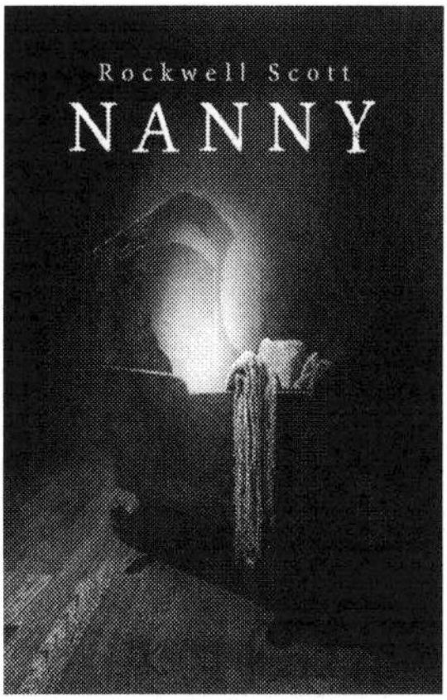

My novella Nanny is FREE and exclusively available to members of my Reader Group.

Go to my website to sign up and download your free ebook today! You'll also be notified when I release new books.

www.rockwellscott.com

A NOTE FROM ROCKWELL

Hey there.

I would like to thank you for spending your valuable time reading my book. I sincerely hope you enjoyed it.

As you may know, reviews are one of the biggest things readers can do to support their favorite authors. They help get the word out and convince potential readers to take a chance on me.

I would like to ask that you consider leaving a review. I would be very grateful, and of course, it is always valuable to me to hear what my readers think of my work.

Thank you in advance to everyone who chooses to do so, and I hope to see you back in my pages soon.

Sincerely,

- Rockwell

ALSO BY ROCKWELL SCOTT

The Tenth Ward

Meet Randolph Casey—university professor by day, demonologist, ghost hunter, and paranormal investigator by night. And he's about to take on his most dangerous assignment.

Rand has seen better days—his ex is getting remarried, and a persistent "non-believing" university auditor is threatening his job. The last thing Rand needs is to take on a new ghost hunting case. But when a desperate couple approaches him about their terminally-ill daughter, Georgia, who claims a ghost is visiting her hospital room at night, he can't seem to turn them away.

Rand figures that banishing Georgia's ghostly intruder will be a routine matter. All he needs to do is guide the lingering ghost to the afterlife. But when the ghost returns with a vengeance, attacking Georgia and terrorizing other hospital wards, Rand realizes this is no benign spirit, but an evil demonic entity. He's faced such monsters before, but never one so complex, so aggressive and violent. If he doesn't unravel its ancient origins and discover how to banish it back to hell, a hospital full of people will fall victim to its destructive agenda.

The Tenth Ward is a supernatural horror thriller for readers who love stories about hauntings and battles with the demonic—the truest form of evil that exists in our world.

ALSO BY ROCKWELL SCOTT

The Gravewatcher

Every night at 3 AM, he visits the graveyard and speaks to someone who isn't there.

Eleanor has created an ideal life for herself in New York City with a career that keeps her too busy, just as she likes it. But when she receives an anonymous message that her estranged brother Dennis is dead, her fast-paced routine grinds to a halt. She rushes to Finnick, Louisiana — the small, backward town where her brother lived and temporarily settles into his creepy, turn-of-the-century house until she can figure out how he died.

But that night, Eleanor spots a young boy in the cemetery behind Dennis's house, speaking to the gravestones. When she approaches him, Eleanor's interruption of the boy's ritual sets off a chain reaction of horror she could have never prepared for. The footsteps, the voices, and the shadowy apparitions are only the beginning.

Eleanor learns that the boy, Walter, is being oppressed by a demonic entity that compels him to visit the graveyard every night. She suspects Dennis also discovered this nightly ritual and tried to stop it, and that is why he died. Because there are others in Finnick who know about Walter's involvement with the evil spirit and want it to continue, and they will do whatever it takes to stop Eleanor from ruining their carefully laid plans. Now Eleanor must finish what her brother started — to rescue the boy from the clutches of hell before he loses his soul forever.

The Gravewatcher is a supernatural horror novel for readers who love stories about haunted houses, creepy graveyards, and battles with the demonic - the truest form of evil that exists in our world.

ABOUT THE AUTHOR

Rockwell Scott is an author of supernatural horror fiction.

When not writing, he can be found working out, enjoying beer and whiskey with friends, and traveling internationally.

Feel free to get in touch!

Facebook
www.facebook.com/rockwellscottauthor

Twitter
@rockwell_scott

www.rockwellscott.com

rockwellscottauthor@gmail.com

Made in the USA
San Bernardino, CA
29 May 2020

72471244R00149